ALSO BY DARCEY BELL

All I Want

Something She's Not Telling Us

A Simple Favor

WOMAN of the YEAR

WOMAN
of the
YEAR

A Novel

DARCEY BELL

EMILY BESTLER BOOKS

ATRIA

New York • London • Toronto • Sydney • New Delhi

EMILY
BESTLER
BOOKS

ATRIA

An Imprint of Simon & Schuster, Inc.
1230 Avenue of the Americas
New York, NY 10020

First Emily Bestler Books/Atria Paperback edition March 2023

EMILY BESTLER BOOKS/ATRIA PAPERBACK and colophon are trademarks of Simon & Schuster, Inc.

For information about special discounts for bulk purchases, please contact Simon & Schuster Special Sales at 1-866-506-1949 or business@simonandschuster.com.

The Simon & Schuster Speakers Bureau can bring authors to your live event. For more information or to book an event, contact the Simon & Schuster Speakers Bureau at 1-866-248-3049 or visit our website at www.simonspeakers.com.

Interior design by Dana Sloan

Manufactured in the United States of America

1 3 5 7 9 10 8 6 4 2

Library of Congress Cataloging-in-Publication Data is available.

ISBN 978-1-9821-7730-0
ISBN 978-1-9821-7732-4 (ebook)

WOMAN
of the
YEAR

Chapter One

THE VIDEO of my cat saving my life was shared over four million times.

Cat lovers and cat haters alike were thrilled by the sight of my large, broad-shouldered gray cat sinking his teeth and claws into my assailant, reducing a full-grown man to a whimpering wreck, curled up on the floor.

In the interviews that fueled my sudden media stardom, I'd say: The film speaks for itself. I focused on Catzilla, his courage, loyalty, and grace, the gentleness beneath his brute strength. The telepathic bond between us.

A few interviewers couldn't help asking, Had I trained my cat to attack?

The answer was no. Of course not! He'd never done anything like that before.

He knew that I was in danger.

He was my protector.

All that publicity led to my current association with the American Feline Protection Society. Really, a second career. A first career, if I'm being honest. So you could say that my cat saved my life in more ways than one.

———

When I tell the story, I keep certain . . . details to myself. Certain things I don't want people knowing, information that might upset my fans and my colleagues at the AFP Society.

For example, the night I poisoned Holly Serpenta.

The Woman of the Year.

I didn't want to kill her. I just wanted to make her sick.

I didn't even want to make her very sick. I just wanted to see her *get* sick in front of two hundred adoring fans who'd paid thousands of dollars to have dinner with her, and who, thanks to me, would be getting more than they paid for.

I didn't want her dead. Well, maybe briefly dead. I wanted to revive her. I wanted to bring her back to life. I considered getting an EpiPen, in case she went into shock. I could *happen* to have one on me.

That might have been hard to explain, seeing as I don't have allergies. Back when men took me out to restaurants, and the waiters asked if I had any food allergies, I'd say, "None that I know of *so far*." Funny joke. The waiters would pretend-laugh. They'd heard it a million times.

You need a prescription to get an EpiPen. It's expensive. The manufacturer went to jail for jacking up the price. But probably no one ever asks why you have a lifesaving drug in your purse. Lorelei, what were you doing with the epinephrine, the Narcan?

I wanted to bring a dead celebrity back to life and say, *Hi, Holly! Remember me?*

Oddly, or not so oddly, someone *did* kill Holly. The Woman of the Year.

Later that same week.

Apparently, I wasn't the only one who wanted her dead.

Not that I wanted her dead. As I keep saying.

I wasn't the one who killed her.

———

Everyone on social media knew that Holly Serpenta's loyal assistants, Tamara and Dan, were always nearby with the rescue hypodermic that would save her in seconds. Not that they'd need to, because they basically tasted every whole grain of gourmet vegan food that passed her lips.

If they'd put me at another table at the Woman of the Year Gala Benefit dinner, anywhere other than smack up against the kitchen door, I might not have gone through with it.

Self-defense versus a swinging door. How would that play in court?

Miss Green, how do you plead?

Not guilty, Your Honor. Every time the kitchen door slammed open, I had to jump up and scoot over to avoid being concussed by a tray of delicacies on their way to another table. Members of the jury, what would the waiter have done if I'd grabbed a nest of puff pastry cradling a fat blip of caviar? He would have smacked my hand away. Or maybe he'd check out my watch—cheap!—and jewelry— cheap!—and then smack my hand away.

The caviar was for the guests who'd "bought" entire tables and invited a dozen rich, famous friends.

By the time a picked-over tray had limped past me, every last micro fish egg was gone, and the soggy pastry cups exuded a pinkish salmon paste.

The waiter's smile had been superior and triumphantly bitchy.

I'd smiled and shaken my head no, my Barbie wig shifting a little on my head. Thanks, but no thanks!

———

At the *very* least, I would have been sent away somewhere for psychiatric observation. The judge would have been right. I was temporarily out of my mind.

So what if I'd spent forty years being sane, holding down a job, paying rent, having boyfriends then not having boyfriends, taking care of my cats—one cat at a time—nursing them in their final illnesses, nursing my parents in *their* final illnesses. Living a life.

Not drunk in a gutter. Not in a psychiatric unit. Not a crack whore.

I get credit for that. Considering.

Still . . . I must have been crazy, after all those years, to poison the *partly* guilty person instead of the *really* guilty person.

Of course I had a good excuse: the *really* guilty person was dead.

A good excuse, not a great one.

———

Welcome to the annual Woman of the Year Gala Benefit.

Why, thank you. Great to be here.

The long, narrow restaurant was jammed full of women swimming in slo-mo through a body-temperature sea of perfumes so expensive that the scents weren't competing, though the women certainly were. Who was the most famous, the prettiest, the best dressed, the most respected for her talent, career, and good works?

Mirror, mirror on the wall. Who donated the most money from her women-only hedge fund to an all-women company developing renewable energy options?

It was an A-list crowd of women so famous that even I recognized them. So famous that looking around was like paging through a magazine you'd read if you could afford an eight-hundred-dollar haircut instead of the YouTube video of a fourteen-year-old telling you how to cut the perfect bangs that she definitely did not cut herself.

There was Chief Justice Sonia Sotomayor with Laurie Anderson, Susan Sarandon, and Miley Cyrus. And what was Gwyneth Paltrow whispering to Zadie Smith?

I don't remember who sat at my table. I didn't recognize any of them. The Z-list guests couldn't look at each other. I'd thought I was above all that because I was on a secret mission. Then why did I feel like I'd swallowed an ice cube. My back and shoulders were so frozen solid I couldn't turn my head. If I'd tried to smile—*Hi, nice to meet you. I'm Miranda DeWitt, and you are . . . ?*—my face would have shattered like glass.

For starters, I'm not Miranda DeWitt.

———

I was sure that everyone was looking at me, except that no one was looking at me, which—for the women in that room—was worse than everyone looking at them. They *wanted* everyone looking at them. That was the point.

How would I start a conversation? *Are you a fan of Holly's? Of, you know . . . this year's Woman of the Year? Oh, I see. They gave out extra tickets to this dinner at your office?*

And me? Oh, I've known Holly forever.

Holly and I are friends from college.

———

The first part of the evening went okay. I'd dressed up . . . in costume. The costume of a woman with money, self-respect, and social position.

I didn't really think Holly would recognize me, though I was vain enough to *secretly* think she might. I didn't think anyone would remember having seen me at the dinner. Dressing up was more of a magical-thinking thing. I wanted to be someone else.

Not me. Not Lorelei Green. Not Lorelei Green, Long Island born, college dropout, forty, currently unemployed, formerly an underpaid, overworked human resources "counselor." The giver of pink slips, the wisher of *goodbye and good luck.*

I'd spent years inflicting and observing unemployment pain I could do nothing about. I hated firing people. I told myself I was making a bad experience less painful. Also I needed a job. Every so often I applied for other jobs and didn't get them and gave up too soon. Bookstores didn't pay enough, nor did movie concession stands; two places I would have liked to work.

Go ahead and judge me if you have never done anything out of laziness and because you needed the money.

———

My hope was that I was making bad things better because I am an empath. I feel more than the average person. I feel what others are feeling. Sometimes too intensely. I've always known what my cats were feeling. More rarely, other people, though that would have helped me if I'd become a therapist, which I'd originally wanted.

You may wonder how an empath could want to sicken and publicly embarrass an innocent celebrity who had been her college friend.

First: my former friend wasn't innocent.

Second: she was never my friend.

And third: just because empaths know what a person is feeling doesn't mean they want to make that person feel better.

———

In the biopic based on my life, my first post-college jobs (actually, dropped-out-of-college jobs) would flash onto the screen. Waitress. *Flash!* Fired. Sales clerk. *Flash!* Fired. Nursery school aide. *Flash!* Quit. I thought I could clean up toddler shit, but I couldn't.

I put on the last good clothes I had and got a job as a receptionist at Cobrox Inc. After twenty years, I still can't explain what Cobrox does, though I asked (and have been asked) many times, and I'm not stupid. It's like an agent, or middleman, a corporate matchmaker. The company sets up meetings about purchasing for large industrial buyers. The supply chain. I assume my failure to "get it" was why I wound up firing people who "got it" less than I did.

I'd done other jobs at the company, secretarial mostly. Low-level managerial. Then the human resources person in charge of laying people off quit. Someone thought I'd be good at it, which I was, if *good-at-it* meant that no one showed up at the office with an assault weapon.

Now Cobrox no longer needed me. They announced furloughs and terminations electronically. They fired me via email.

The office had grown more robotic. People spoke in scripts, like telemarketers and hotline volunteers.

By the night of the Woman of the Year dinner, my unemployment benefits were about to expire. From the outside, my situation must have looked desperate.

Maybe because of my uncertain present, I was more interested in the past, which I had tried to forget.

———

Is it fair? Two girls from the same college class, one rich, famous, and well respected.

Introducing: Holly Serpenta. The Woman of the Year.

The other one was me, Lorelei Green, recently fired from her shitty corporate job of firing other people.

Maybe you think I have blood on my hands. The blood of the newly unemployed. But I wasn't the one who shed it. I had to harden, cell by cell, which hurts, like any surgery you do on yourself.

———

I'd bought the ticket to the Woman of the Year dinner with my personal credit card. I'm not a criminal. But when it said, *Name of Guest*, I typed in: *Miranda DeWitt*.

Not me.

Imaginary Miranda: the plucky survivor of an ugly divorce. My alter ego would be fine when the dust settled, but the poor thing was struggling. The gala-benefit ticket site didn't care who was buying and who was attending, as long as the charges cleared. They cared that I wasn't a robot. A robot was making sure that I wasn't another robot. What a joy it would be to say, *Can you keep a secret? I'm a robot too!*

Not that I am a robot.

I found, in the back of my closet, a lightly worn pair of shoes that Minnie Mouse would wear if she were rich and had the ankles for five-inch heels. I'd bought them in a resale shop. Sometimes I bought things for myself as if I were another person. Without knowing it, I'd shopped for Miranda DeWitt.

Were they the smartest footwear for committing a crime? Who would suspect a woman in vintage Marc Jacobs heels?

They'd remember the shoes and not me. That's what they say in mystery novels and TV detective procedurals. The clever criminal wears an eye-catching accessory—the age-inappropriate kitty-cat headband, the giant aviator glasses, the diamond-studded nose ring—so everyone remembers that, and not her face.

No one sees your shoes in a crowded room. But these women knew what your shoes cost. They could feel it through their feet.

———

Obviously, my decision to poison the Woman of the Year wasn't spur-of-the-moment. It was not about getting a "bad" table at a benefit dinner.

This was about an old crime, about justice, about righting an old wrong. Not perfect justice. The crime was worse than the punishment.

I personally hate the word *revenge*, but I'll let it float there.

The most shameful part—at this gala event celebrating *female power*—is that the crime was about a man.

Partly about a man.

The crime was about a man and a cat.

Mostly about a cat.

The women at the benefit dinner might have better understood about the cat.

———

I decided on a simple black dress (Max Mara—also resale) with a high neck and long, bell-shaped sleeves. I had it dry-cleaned to get rid of the mothball smell.

Dry cleaning isn't cheap. The old man who handed me the ghost dress, swinging in its plastic skin, said, "Going to a party, young lady?"

Young lady? I will never do business there again. I will walk blocks if I have to.

I wore black stockings with the black party dress, and (for luck) my mother's real pearls. Eight dollars bought a pair of secondhand Chanel glasses with turquoise frames in a thrift shop on Second Avenue. No one buys eyeglasses secondhand. They practically pay you to take them.

And then there was the wig. I would have loved wearing a rainbow birthday-clown fuzzball, just for shits and giggles.

I had to go blond. It would be an acceptably diverse crowd, but safety dictated a silvery-blond Barbie bob. When I imagined Miranda, I pictured her brave, worried face.

Maybe the imaginary husband had left Miranda DeWitt for the imaginary young secretary, but Miranda hadn't fallen apart, Miranda got her hair done. Under the wig, I *had* fallen apart, if the sign of falling apart was not getting your hair done.

I used to have great hair. I used to be blond. A blond. I was blond when I knew Holly Serpenta, now the Woman of the Year, when she and I were students at Woodward University.

My hair was gold, and now it's straw. Like Rumpelstiltskin backwards.

———

Back then she was Holly Snopes. For three years of college, I was Laura Lee Green.

Then I was Lorelei.

And now she's Holly Serpenta. What kind of name is that? Name is destiny, really. Like Doctor Pain the dentist. Serpenta is the perfect name for a snake in the grass. The Snake in the Grass of the Year Award. No one calls it that.

In a fairy tale, I would be the witch crashing the royal baby's christening. I would cast the spell that it would take the whole fairy tale to undo.

Chapter Two

OUR FIRST year of college started late because of 9/11. Everyone was nervous. Students were stranded all over the country. That wasn't my problem. Western Massachusetts was a four-hour car ride from my parents' split-level in Sayville.

We students were pretty shell-shocked, and I guess we stayed that way. We were glad to be at a school famous for its psychology department. That was why we'd applied. Some of the school's endowment came from celebrity psychiatrists. It was known to be a good college for the student considering a future as a therapist or psychiatrist or in any of the helping professions.

Supposedly Sigmund Freud had lunch with the president of Woodward College en route to Clark University nearby, where he'd actually given a couple of lectures. The Woodward brochure had a picture of Freud in it, to make people think he'd taught there.

Psychology majors—I was one—were required to take a Freud course. The entire course was about how Freud got everything wrong. Special attention was paid to the lectures he'd given at Clark, and how pointless they were. It wasn't that the psych department was totally anti-Freud, but a powerful faction at our school found Freud less than . . . useful.

Our department emphasized conditioning and behavior modification.

Our professors were more likely to attract generous government funding. The behaviorists referred to the few Freudians on the faculty as mentalists, which I found confusing, because I'd grown up thinking that a mentalist was a mind reader in old-fashioned vaudeville theater.

The Freud (that is, the anti-Freud) course was taught by the department chair, Professor Otto Muller, who had studied at Harvard with the distinguished behavioral scientist B. F. Skinner, who was the subject of another required course. To Professor Muller, Skinner—who designed the box with a lever that rats learned to pull to get food—was a god.

Professor Muller told his classes that it was untrue, a wicked anti-behaviorist lie, that Skinner raised his children in boxes equipped with levers that doled out unhealthy candy-colored cereal snacks.

Like any new idea, behaviorism had enemies who wanted to destroy it.

The college's reputation reassured parents, especially after 9/11 when the world seemed topsy-turvy, that even if we went off the rails at school, there were famous psychologists around to guide us. And the Berkshires seemed like a safe place to be in case of another attack.

———

The buildings and grounds at Woodward had belonged to the richest family that Edith Wharton knew. Jeremy Vernon Woodward, whose family was in timber, mining, and importing shea butter and coconut oil, had built a compound on the model of Versailles, where his parents had taken him once as a child. The central granite castle was flanked by shepherds' cottages, farm buildings, and an Italianate concert hall.

In the main building, the Hall of Mirrors had been converted into a line of windowed offices. Many classrooms had mirrors—in some cases, one-way mirrors. But a long, mirrored corridor seemed excessive, forcing self-conscious college kids to watch themselves walking to class.

By the time the Woodward estate was deeded to the college, there was one Woodward daughter left. She and her astronomer husband had an autistic son who had been greatly helped by a doctor from Vienna: our own Professor Muller's father.

The boy's mother moved to France after her son drowned in the mansion's magnificent swimming pool, which was decorated like an Egyptian bath. No one ever used the pool. There was no Woodward swim team. The pool was said to be haunted. Every fall, a few brave swimmers tried it out, and there was another sighting, another ghostly presence, and people stopped going.

I don't really like the film *Cat People*, but I watch it over and over. I hate how it portrays cats as savage beasts drenched in human bloodlust. Still, I get a thrill watching the watery shadow of the murderous cat ripple across the tiled wall of the indoor pool.

———

As far as I know, no one went off the rails because of 9/11. Was the school a safe place? It depended on who you were, whom you met, and what classes you took.

If our parents had known what went on there, especially in

some of our psych classes, they wouldn't have breathed those big doggy sighs of relief when they drove off and left us outside our dorms.

Even if our families knew, what could they have done? The psychology department was the pride of the school. The psych professors—even the teaching assistants—pretty much did what they wanted.

Professor Muller was a frequent guest at the White House during both Bush administrations. Yet every Monday at noon he stood at the bottom of Franklin Hall and taught Intro to Psych 101. Such was his commitment to teaching, and also to research. We often stayed up late studying. Normally noon was our nap time, especially when they dimmed the lights to show slides. But we stayed awake in Professor Muller's class. We felt that he was testing us, studying us, even in the dark with the light from the slides and films—photos of Freud and Jung and Skinner, videos of rats running mazes—flashing on our faces.

Sometimes, if you drifted off during one of his lectures, Professor Muller would say something that woke you, and you'd have the strangest feeling, as if he knew what you were thinking. What you'd been daydreaming about. It was as if he'd gotten inside your head. As if he'd read your mind.

Many students in the college and graduate school had work-study jobs in his laboratory. At one point the number of caged rats pulling levers was so high that the noise was said to be deafening. People said that being in the lab felt like being on a factory floor or in a busy machine shop.

We called Professor Muller "the Nazi." We had no idea whether he had been a Nazi or not. For all we knew, he was a refugee from the Nazis. We were young and careless. But he dressed like an

Austrian aristocrat from central casting, with an ivory-headed cane and a dueling scar down his cheek. And an eye patch. When someone overdoes a certain part, you wonder if it's real.

People said that both eyes were fine, that he wore the patch for effect. He took it off to flirt with female graduate students at the department Christmas parties. This was when male faculty members did what they wanted. That's how it was at our school, certainly in our department.

Muller had written shelves of books. He'd done important research. He had studied bias, attachment, fear, love, every human emotion. He'd convinced all sorts of important people that you could learn about human beings by starving rats and sleep-depriving monkeys.

He was an expert on motivation, on why people did what they did, which was probably why the government was interested in his research. Today he would have gotten in trouble for his interest in eugenics and for showing the slides of scientists measuring the heads of Indigenous people. Now someone would protest. Twenty years ago, we were silent. We wanted jobs. We wanted futures, not that it's an excuse.

We were frightened of him. Not that he publicly shamed anyone, like law professors on TV. He didn't seem to notice or care that his students were there. We didn't go near him. He wasn't the kind of teacher whose students crowded around him after class.

Sometimes he could have been talking to himself. Once, he gave the same lecture complete with questions, two days in a row. We had no choice. We had to go. The class was a requirement. His grad students took attendance. Also, Professor Muller and his colleagues experimented on human beings. Specifically, on us students. Not in a painful or invasive way. No electrodes taped to our foreheads. Even so, there was damage.

In his course on Skinner, Professor Muller lectured about the Milgram experiment. Obedience to Authority was the official name of the experiment Stanley Milgram conducted at Yale in the 1960s. The subjects were told to deliver electric shocks to an invisible person who was learning something. When that person made mistakes, the subjects were instructed to give stronger shocks, even when they heard the subject howling in pain.

Professor Muller said it was cruel to everyone, pointless to prove what everyone knew. Every war and atrocity should have taught us something about the . . . flaw in the human design.

I remember him saying: "You can't make people better. You could train them not to be worse. But what does *worse* mean?"

I recall him chuckling.

"*Worse* is in the eye of the beholder."

Basically, we students were tuition-paying lab rats.

Graduate students watched certain classes from behind one-way mirrors. They observed us in the dining room, in the library, study rooms, dorms. We were spied on, and we knew it. It was a game to get away with things the grad students didn't notice. Mostly harmless stuff: smoking cigarettes, having parties, drinking in our dorm rooms.

It was not an atmosphere conducive to mental health.

If our parents knew we were being observed, they didn't care. They liked that the college had curb appeal, as they say now on TV. Its rolling lawns were dotted with chapels that doubled as classrooms. There were Gothic follies teeming with bats. The parents liked how Woodward looked like a college in an old movie. A college playing a college. The students liked that too.

I liked college, more or less. For a few months, I liked it a lot.
And then I didn't, at all.

––––––

The most famous—infamous—course at Woodward was Interpersonal Relations (IP) 121. It was basically group therapy, except
that you got a grade and college credit, and no one was helped by
it or better adjusted when it was over. Breakups, breakdowns, and
feuds began in the class. In the real world, you went to therapy
for help with your problems. At Woodward, you took IP 121 to
develop new problems or discover ones you didn't know you had.

Who decided that doctoral candidates could learn from
watching college kids mess with each other's heads? It was like
reality TV, of which I am a fan. But this was real. Unscripted. And
no one was filming. No camera, no crew. More reality, less TV.

For a while, not that long ago, I watched a Japanese TV series
called *Terrace House*. Young non-actors living together, chatting,
flirting, gossiping. Turning on each other. Every so often the scene
changes and we see a group of slightly older professional people
watch tapes of the painful embarrassing shows and giggle and
make comments. Maybe one reason I liked it was that it reminded
me of the graduate students observing our class, or how I imagined them, anyway: laughing. Taking notes.

It might seem strange that a department so devoted to behavior control should take pride in a course that encouraged acting
out. Breaking the rules. There were a few inflexible rules no one
broke. Obviously, no violence or threats. No interrupting or talking over other people. We were told to act *naturally* even though
someone was watching. As if there were anything natural about

a class of college-age strangers telling each other our hopes and fears and dreams.

At the end of the first class, Professor Randall said, "We encourage you to let your feelings happen."

I felt my face flush. He couldn't know what those feelings were.

———

Movie-star blond, I stood out at a college where most of my female classmates had badly cut mouse-colored hair.

It was hard to get into Woodward. You needed the grades, the recommendations, the extracurricular blah blah blah. Why should girl high-school-math geniuses care about good haircuts? Who had the time to look fabulous?

I looked like Miranda DeWitt looked in Miranda DeWitt's dreams. All I had to do was wash my hair and tie it back with a little black bow like Catherine Deneuve in *Belle du Jour*. Catherine Deneuve in *Belle de Jour* was the look I was going for. The perfect French housewife who works at the upscale whorehouse without messing up her hair.

I don't know why I liked that film. Maybe because of the nasty relationship I had with my high school chess-champion boyfriend.

In college, Holly Serpenta, then Snopes, our current Woman of the Year, had been one of Cinderella's mice. And now she was Cinderella, proof of what can be done with camera-ready highlights, filler, Botox, round-the-clock makeup artists, and an expensive haircut.

I'd been popular in high school. I'd been a cheerleader in tenth grade. In the new life that began in college, none of that had happened. Nor had I spent my senior year of high school having bad, semi-rough, semi-consensual sex with the chess champion—after school, in his bedroom or mine, when our parents were at work. Consensual, for sure. Or mostly. It was like an after-school job I had a few times a week.

I started over in college. My past was more or less erased. I even changed my name to Lorelei at the end of junior year.

The truth is: My name was changed for me. By my abuser.

It feels good to call him that.

Chapter Three

*D*RESSING FOR the Woman of the Year Gala, I went for the Upper East Side divorcée. Poor Miranda! Dumped for the secretary, but she'll do fine in the settlement.

On the subway from my apartment in Brooklyn Heights to the dinner at the South of Saigon restaurant, my disguise was working. I felt that strangers were looking at me and seeing Miranda.

Nearer the venue, I got concerned. But the four men in black suits flanking the restaurant door—bouncers? guards?—were fine with it. They weren't judging my fashion sense, my hotness, my disposable income, but just the likelihood of my not having a ticket, or smelling bad, or making trouble.

"Enjoy your evening, ma'am," one said.

Ma'am was kindly meant. Really, it signified nothing. I was not going to let it throw me.

Two beautiful young women, coltish as baby giraffes in black dresses half the size of mine, leaned over the reception lectern. I stopped breathing while the friendlier one searched for Miranda's name on her tablet.

Scrolling, scrolling.

Holding my breath.

There it was! Big grin of relief and welcome. Exhale.

Hi, Miranda!

I hoped her tablet didn't say that I was one of the guests for whom someone bought a single ticket. Someone named Lorelei Green had bought it for Miranda as a cheer-up present. A chance to see the inspiring Holly Serpenta, whom Miranda admired.

The rich donors who purchased whole tables or the bold-faced celebrity bling probably had stars beside their names on the tablets. I hoped giraffe-girl's tablet didn't mention that Lorelei Green bought her friend Miranda the cheapest seat. No way of her knowing that even that ridiculous expense severely dented Lorelei Green's bank account. No possibility of her suspecting how close Lorelei Green's Amex card was to being maxed out.

Attitude was essential.

The young woman took a little card and scribbled my table number on it: 8.

Eight seemed promising. The important thing was proximity to the honoree. That was too much to hope for, but a decent sight line would do.

Both girls said, "Enjoy your evening."

Enjoy your evening. Enjoy your evening.

Thank you.

I wove toward the bar, past guests air-kissing and flapping like waterbirds. Slipping business cards into purses, typing numbers into phones. Making appointments. Someone said, "God! You look amazing, I haven't seen you since that endless snooze of a board meeting." I heard a few women say, "Congratulations, that's great." They sounded almost sorry that someone else was being congratulated. Not sorry, exactly. Just disappointed.

People glanced at me just long enough to see if I was someone they should know, and then past me, looking for someone who was.

I could have been part of the wallpaper, patterned with the lush foliage of a steamy jungle plantation. You'd think this crowd would have a problem with the *Heart of Darkness* decor, but they were saving their outrage for something bigger than wallpaper. Or maybe I was the only one looking at the walls.

I looked around, I looked around.

I saw her.

Holly Serpenta. The Woman of the Year.

She was down at the far end of the room, but you couldn't miss the popping flashbulbs. She stood there, composed, with a frozen perfect smile as the cameras rattled like machine guns.

She looked amazing. I was glad I'd spent so much time internet-stalking her. It made it easier to see her in person. Like an animated online photo. Twenty years had aged her, but not a teensy fraction of how much those years had aged me.

I'd started out as the pretty one. The girl most likely. Now *she* was the star. It was like a fairy tale in which the witch masquerades as the princess and *gets away with it*. That never happens in fairy tales! The witch always loses, and the princess is restored to her throne.

I wanted Holly's clothes. I wanted her shoes. I wanted her fame, her money, her jewelry, her first husband—the handsome heir to the Italian glove fortune. I wanted her widowhood, and then I wanted her second husband—the retired diplomat and race car fan who also died tragically young. I wanted her two gorgeous half-Italian kids, her shelter-magazine apartment. The shelter-magazine cover of her apartment. I even wanted her Connecticut farmhouse. I wanted her success. I wanted her teeth. Her haircutter, her colorist, her cosmetic surgeon.

I had come to that moment, in the middle of the journey of my life. The point where I wanted what she had—and I knew I would never have it.

Go ahead and judge me, you people who have never once in your life wanted something that someone else had.

―――

When I finally worked my way to the bar, I felt like I did in Interpersonal Relations 121, the class that the Woman of the Year and I took together, our senior year in college.

Where we'd met.

I remembered that feeling of not knowing what to say, how to jump in. By the time I broke into the class discussion, everyone had moved on to another subject.

Actually, I never finished the class.

That was for other reasons.

Until then, I'd never been shy about talking in class. That's why I did so well in high school and my first three years of college. I could talk. I wasn't afraid. But I'd never been in a class in which you said something, and then the next person asked *why* you'd said it, what you *really* meant, how it made you feel, how it made *them* feel, how it made *everyone* feel, and so on.

What reminded me of that at the gala was how hard it was to order a drink. Beautiful people cut in front of me, requesting obscure cocktails that the proud bartenders could definitely do but which took forever muddling the orange peel. No one was rushed, everyone got served, enjoy your evening, enjoy your evening, but it was never my turn to have a delicious drink and enjoy my evening.

By the time I ordered, someone was ringing a bell. *Ding ding! Go to your table!* I asked for a bourbon on the rocks.

The bartender looked like a '70s TV star. You don't often see that Elvis look, at least not on men. He was handsome, which was maybe why I started babbling, though I was beyond caring about his good looks or good opinion.

I said, "I don't usually drink. I pretty much stopped completely. But this is a special occasion. I'm so excited to see Holly."

Too much information. Did he think that I was trying to keep him pouring? That trick worked better when I was young and hot. Now it often backfired. Now they were more likely to stop pouring and stare at me until I shut up.

"Bourbon? You got it," the bartender said. He had no idea who Holly was. Holly was a paycheck. It was a comfort, his not knowing. He *knew* I was lying about not drinking. Who says, "I don't drink, but I'd like a bourbon on the rocks?" As if he cared!

The first sip helped. I felt the edge of well-being the first drink gives me, until the second drink reminds me of all the little things wrong with the world, and the third makes me think about all the big things wrong with my life, and the fourth drink makes me slightly unsteady, and the fifth makes me want to smack someone. Which is why I don't drink. In public.

A few sips would do the trick tonight.

I started at the front, looking for table 8. That is, I started near Holly. I kept my back to her. She wouldn't have recognized me, even without the wig. But that wasn't why I pretended not to see her. I wanted to seem like a person who knows the celebrity is *standing right there* but is too cool to stare. Unlike the fans who whip out their phones and plead for a selfie and then make that cringe-y smile for the camera.

Was I stalking Holly? Are you stalking someone if you're not looking at her? Yes, if you always know where she is. Are lovers stalking each other when their eyes meet across the crowded room?

The table numbers weren't in order. I couldn't find 8. I wandered around, bumping into people, until I found one of the baby-giraffe girls. I asked where table 8 was. She was no longer my best friend as she pointed toward the kitchen door.

That's when I thought, *Let's do this*. Still, I had to play it by ear. If one element was missing, if anything seemed *off*, I'd try again another time. I wasn't planning to go to jail and make Holly even more famous for having survived an attack. By me.

The Woman of the Year led a public life. It wasn't hard to find her. Maybe she'd be Woman of the Year next year too. *If* she was free that night.

I needed to concentrate. I left my empty glass of ice cubes and alcohol-tinged water on a table at which no one had sat down yet and looked for table 8.

Everyone was a star. Everyone but me and my tablemates. Who were we?

Two newly divorcing struggling blonds, one of them (me) an unemployed human resources worker pretending to be a newly divorcing struggling blond.

Two silent, sour, middle-aged couples.

Three gender-fluid recent college grads, all (I imagined) celebrity personal assistants. They were the only ones who smiled at me, but they were too far away to talk, which was just as well, considering why I was there. Free food and wine was fine with them.

There were three empty seats at my table. I envied the no-shows who had something better to do.

A lot of planning had gone into this. Not just the wig and the outfit but the walnut oil.

Ah, yes. The walnut oil.

———

Everyone knew everything about the Woman of the Year. We knew about her tantrums, and the costly apology-presents she gave the victims of her flameouts. We knew where she got her clothes (free) and where she got her highlights done (also free).

We knew about her allergies. She was on the board of the Nut Allergy Awareness Foundation. Everyone who'd been to the dentist knew how she'd gotten sick on an airplane and nearly died, and how the kindly (first-class) flight attendant shot her up with an EpiPen and saved her life and avoided an expensive lawsuit. The flight attendant was a hero.

Now Holly Serpenta not only carried an EpiPen in her purse but she did public service TV announcements for the evil drug company that made it, which meant she got hers for free, though she was one of the few who could afford it.

Did I know about her allergy in college? If people were allergic then, they were mostly allergic to cats.

I knew she wasn't allergic to cats, because I'd had a cat. Pyewacket. My first cat. Traditionally, that was the name of a witch's familiar. A witchy name for a sweet kitty who couldn't have been less demonic.

Holly (Snopes, then) and my cat loved each other.

Pyewacket. My first cat. You never forget your first.

Since then I've always had cats. I think it's one reason I so rarely got swiped on dating apps. I talked about my cat too much.

My current cat, Catzilla, was in all my dating-app photos.

In my profile I explained I'd called him that because in certain lights his silvery fur has a greenish tinge and because, even as a kitten in the shelter, he had enormous hunky shoulders. He wasn't really a monster then, but he'd grown into one physically. Sure he was big, but his personality couldn't have been more gentle. Anyway, Catzilla scared guys off, even guys who had cats. There were plenty of single women out there. Who needed to date a woman who led with her monster cat? Who wanted to date a woman who *had* a monster cat?

When I googled "crazy cat lady," it said:

A crazy cat lady can have one cat. Or zero cats. A cat lady can be a man.

That wasn't much help, but further search confirmed what I knew. The phrase really wasn't about the *cats* at all but about the *crazy lady*. About the dubious sanity of an unmarried woman.

Witches were serious cat ladies, and we all know what happened to them.

I'd named my cat Pyewacket. Maybe I was asking for trouble.

Dear Pyewacket, I'm so sorry I didn't name you something else.

———

Masterpieces have been written about cats. The most honest and beautiful book I know is Bohumil Hrabal's *All My Cats*. The Czech writer had a lot of them, some of them were feral. Another favorite is Haruki Murakami's *Kafka on the Shore*, about a man who can talk to cats, who works finding lost cats, and has a special relationship with an intelligent cat named Mimi. Another is *The Cat*, by Colette, about a man who loves his cat more than he loves his wife.

I read and reread a wicked Patricia Highsmith story about a cat and a man who try to kill each other because they are rivals for the same woman. A Siamese cat is locked in a death match with his rival, his owner's boyfriend. First the man tries to throw the cat off a boat, and then the cat arranges the man's fatal fall from a terrace.

That was not what happened with any of my cats.

Catzilla was protecting me. He did what he had to do.

———

Two women—one fictional, one real—who had an excessive number of cats have ruined things for the rest of us. One is Edie Beale, in *Grey Gardens*, who had, along with her mother, fifty-two cats in their decaying Long Island mansion. The other was Eleanor Abernathy, on *The Simpsons*, the lawyer-doctor who burns out and has a glass of wine with her cat, Buster, then gets a second cat and, overnight, is haggard and feral, living with "a few dozen" cats and throwing cats at Lisa. In that episode, Eleanor's screaming, cat-hurling attack flips back to the young Eleanor saying, "I want to be a lawyer and a doctor because a woman can do anything."

Eleanor Abernathy would have loved being Woman of the Year.

Eleanor's plan hadn't worked out.

I felt Eleanor's pain. But this is not that story.

———

Catzilla is huge and beautiful. The video of him fighting off my attacker is the one that everyone knows, but my favorite film clips are of him just stretching lazily on the floor in a beam of morning sunlight. Not that my apartment is all that bright, but cats know how to find the light and warmth. My mother had a brother I loved, my uncle Al, who was old by the time I knew him. He would sit in the perfect chair at the perfect moment for the light to hit his thick, beautiful white hair.

Once I went out on a date with a guy who was very interested in the part of my profile about my cat. He told me about an artist whose work he'd seen, an installation of photos of her cat performing oral sex on her. Had I ever done anything like that? Had I thought about it? He said maybe it sounded a little gross, but you never know till you try it, right? The important thing is to be open.

All this was while we were still having drinks! I got up and ran all the way home.

I don't have to apologize for having had closer and warmer relationships with my cats than I've had with another human being. A list of my reasons could go on for pages.

Cats surprise you but they don't disappoint you.

Cats never scare you. Or almost never. You don't want to step on their tail in the dark.

If cats love you, they never stop loving you. If they run away, it's not about you but about being cats and wanting their freedom.

Cats don't compete with you.

Cats don't tell you what to read.

Cats communicate clearly. They let you know what they want.

Cats never try to make you think that you are losing your mind.

———

Like most pet owners, I have done a lot of thinking about human beings and animals, what they share and how they differ.

No other animal, besides humans, wants to be rich and famous. No other animal is envious and upset because they're not a celebrity.

———

Holly has a dedicated Instagram page on her work for the allergy foundation. Forty thousand asthmatics and their moms follow her. Food corporations have donated generously, mostly peanut butter manufacturers trying to clean up their image.

I found a pharmacist with time on his hands, in an under-populated drugstore on the Lower East Side. I put on makeup and a low-cut shirt and told him about my imaginary mushroom-hunting country friend, always picking iffy mushrooms and nearly dying. Wasn't there something that could make her puke them right up? No, there wasn't. The old gold standard, ipecac, was hard to get and dangerous. I'd be better off running red lights and get-ting her to the ER. The guy was not very bright, and a little naïve, not to wonder why I wanted to make someone puke.

According to the internet, the best method is to administer large quantities of mustard. But a quart of mustard might have been hard to conceal at a catered gala dinner.

That's when I thought of nuts. Peanuts? Too obvious. Ca-shews? Oily. Even I didn't like them. Walnut oil? How elegant, how . . . French. How . . . Holly.

But how was I going to go over to her table and drip walnut oil onto her salad?

I thought I'd seen a detective procedural in which something like that happened. That's the thing about procedurals, you're not supposed to remember. They're like good guests. They entertain you, and then they leave, and you don't have to think about them again.

Guests on your TV screen. I can't remember the last time I had a guest who wasn't on television. I know it might sound a little sad, but sometimes I like to imagine that me and the TV detectives are sharing a couple of bottles of wine.

———

I practiced for weeks, then months. A clean syringe (stolen for a one-night stand years ago, and kept in case I ever needed it) filled with oil and taped to the inside of my arm. (Long sleeves a must!) I practiced with lettuce leaves. I only needed a few drops. I went through gallons of walnut oil—not cheap! I had to find the subtlest brand with the biggest punch, one that wouldn't announce its presence until it was too late.

Yum. Delicious. What was that funny taste . . . ?

Gasp gasp.

Choke.

Vomit!

Probably you have noticed how often people vomit on TV. The rookie cop and the reporter at the crime scene and later the autopsy room. Characters vomit because they're drunk or upset, hungover or carsick. When they hear shocking news. Once you see it, you can't unsee it. I've started saying it out loud. Every time someone throws up on the TV, I say, "Vomit!"

Catzilla gives me a strange look, but I can't help it. It's become a tic.

Maybe that's why I got fixated on making Holly get sick at her Woman of the Year dinner. If things went as planned, would I say "Vomit!" when she did?

It would be smarter not to.

I worried that this would be the one night when she forgot her

EpiPen. But that wouldn't happen. She had assistants to remember what she forgot.

No one remembered me.

———

I knew the tickets hadn't sold out because I'd read about the dinner—and the fact that Holly was this year's honoree—when I got a semi-spam email in my Promotions box that said "Selling Out Fast." An obvious lie. How did I get on their list? I used to donate—not much, but something—to the ACLU.

I'm not a believer. But I did believe that something—call it a Higher Power, as they say in the AA meetings I really should be attending—meant this to happen.

You think you forget, but you don't. You think you forgive, but you don't.

Chapter Four

ON MY plate was a program, with a shiny Christmas-red cover.

11th ANNUAL WOMAN IN POWER DINNER
HONORING HOLLY SERPENTA

The left side listed the donors by contribution. The biggest were the food corporations and Big Pharma. Didn't Holly have a problem with opioids buying her dinner?

On the right was the list of speakers, followed by the menu. Welcome: Sandra Blaine, Acting Director of Women for Women for Women. Introduction: Gloria Steinem.

Tributes . . . I counted six.

This could go on forever.

Acceptance speech: Holly Serpenta.

Spring Capriccio Salad. Salmon al Limone. Parmesan Cream Toast à la Russe.

Hello? Hello? Someone was tapping the microphone.

It's hard to get the crowd's attention when everyone has so

much to say they can't shut up. Only I had nothing to say. I didn't know what to do with my face. Smile, don't smile, look distant, look bored. I turned my chair around to watch a sparrow-woman in an electric-blue suit and a ton of clunky Indigenous jewelry flicking the microphone.

"I'm here to introduce someone who needs no introduction. Maybe less of an introduction than anyone in the world."

Less than Jesus? Less than Charlie Manson?

Gloria Steinem took the microphone. She was smaller and slighter than I imagined, but charming. Impossible to dislike. She talked about how hard it had been to make men listen to women, but now women were listening to women, and some of those women were speaking tonight.

Everyone applauded. Some people jumped up, but by the time I stood, everyone was sitting down again. I couldn't see if my tablemates stood because my back to was to them, but I heard chairs scrape. I hadn't dared to jump up in my five-inch Minnie Mouse heels.

Should I explain I had a back problem? Lying was bad luck. Besides, no one cared. Everyone was applauding.

The first speaker looked like that famous Afghan girl in the photo from the 1980s. The most famous Afghan girl ever, even if no one knew her name. This one's name was Maryam. Her headscarf was a perfect robin's-egg blue, and it floated over her black hair and down onto her flowing dress of the same blue shot with silver.

In perfect lilting English, over a flawless sound system, she explained that she had lost her family during a drone strike and was stranded in a refugee camp when Holly Serpenta rescued her. It was a miracle. Praise God.

Of course Holly picked that girl. Or did everyone in the camp look like a movie star and speak perfect English?

Beautiful Maryam was only one of the women whom Holly had lifted up.

The next young woman, also beautiful, but differently, was skinny, butch, in jeans and red platform shoes, a ripped white T-shirt, a Marlon Brando motorcycle jacket.

Suralyn Taylor, Harvard PhD candidate.

"In my elementary school," she said, "this was our math lesson: If one joint costs five bucks, how much can you charge a second-grader for a half ounce of weed? And then Holly came along and started the after-school girls' club, and we were, like, all playing chess."

Why did the word *chess* cause a ripple of awkward laughter?

"Holly's foundation paid for tutors and then college, and now I've done everything but my thesis in physics at Harvard."

Physics? Harvard? Wow.

My heart was the only heart that hardened with every tragedy Holly fixed. Was I the only one whose tragedy she'd *caused*? Next we heard from a battered wife, a person you couldn't imagine hurting, she seemed so easily broken. But now she was whole. Holly had glued her back together.

Flapping her hand to ward off the swell of applause, Holly approached the mike, pausing for long hugs with the previous speakers.

I hardly heard her speech. She could never have accomplished what she'd accomplished without all the women she listed. The crowd applauded each name. She said she wasn't really Woman of the Year, because all women were the woman of the year, all sharing their struggles and triumphs.

She spoke for twenty minutes. Unbelievable! On and on about her successes, her virtues, the obstacles she'd overcome, the famous people—plenty of A-list names dropped here—all the dear friends who'd been so helpful. She smiled in all the right places. Her eyes welled with tears at the perfect moments.

She told a long, rambling story about how she found Maryam in the refugee camp, then listed by name the heroic doctors and nurses who worked there. Things lightened up a little when she described—also at extreme length—the run-down conditions and prisonlike vibe of Suralyn's school, and how little by little everything changed when even the toughest girls got into chess. And about all the battered and abused women finding a place to stay and get help.

I glanced around the restaurant. Everyone seemed enchanted. Could I really have been the only one in that room who wanted to kill her? She had done so much good in the world. I had done less than nothing. The point was that she had done something *to me*.

Not that I wanted to kill her.

I fought off the panicky thought that she would never stop talking, that I had gone to hell without knowing it and I would be stuck here forever listening to Holly. I kept thinking it was over, that she had run out of things to say about herself. But the pause was Holly coming up for air before starting again about what a goddess she was.

The standing ovation was helpful. I could slip away and head toward the front of the room. Excuse me, excuse me. I edged my way through the crowd around Holly, who had returned to her table. I waited for my moment when she spotted me. Was she wondering if she knew me? Even if I wasn't in disguise, she would never have excavated the college beauty from under the wreckage. Something must have struck a chord, because her gaze caught mine, and she waved me over.

I said, "I'm sure you don't remember me. I was in your graduate class at Columbia."

I'd never gone to Columbia, but I knew that Holly had.

"Of course!" Holly prided herself, publicly, on never forgetting a face.

Among the reasons I couldn't use my real name was that she'd tried to get in touch with me, the real me, Lorelei Green, two years ago.

She'd wanted me to confirm her #MeToo story.

She got as far as my personal email.

I didn't answer.

I knew that she wasn't going to tell the real story.

The part about me and my cat.

Pyewacket.

"Miranda DeWitt," I said.

Miranda DeWitt was taking a risk. Would she recognize the name of a girl we went to school with? A girl who'd achieved some celebrity by dying tragically young?

The name rang a bell for Holly, but the ringing faded. She'd heard too many names since then. She couldn't take any more names in, unless they were famous.

"I was Miranda Cottle then. Miss Serpenta—"

"Call me Holly," she interrupted.

"I am such a fan. I am so honored to meet you. Could I take just one picture for my husband and daughter? She worships you."

I have no husband, and if I had a daughter, she wouldn't worship Holly.

After a beat Holly said, "Sure. Can I trust you not to post it on social media? I hate that. Don't you?"

"Sure." I would hate that, too, if it ever happened.

I leaned toward her, over her salad, and I discharged my little jet of walnut oil.

She held still and flashed me her practiced social smile. I leaned in for a close-up. Snap snap. I'd shot the walnut oil onto her salad. I pretended to take her picture. I didn't actually take it. I didn't want it on my phone

Thank you. This will mean so much.

She'd already lost interest in me, not that she had had any.

I returned to my table and waited. A professional assassin would have left the dinner, leaving nothing behind but a memory of Minnie Mouse shoes. But I was an amateur. I wanted to see what would happen.

I waited and watched. Holly, too, was waiting, though she didn't know it.

Chapter Five

INTERPERSONAL Relations 121. We weren't allowed to take the class until our junior year. Maybe they thought that if we were older and more mature—more secure—there was less chance of our being damaged by the group-theory fireworks that might explode in the classroom. Even if we were damaged, we'd be their problem for less time.

That was the class's reputation. Enroll at your own risk.

Naturally, a hundred students always applied for ten places.

It was a glamour experience, something we'd heard about, unique to Woodward College. It was the kind of thing you'd want to talk about later. That, at least, turned out to be true. I'm talking about it now.

Admission to the class was by interview. The teacher, or facilitator, as they called it, got to choose the students. There was a different facilitator every year.

Most of the younger faculty wanted to teach the class. Several had written papers based on their observations about the group, articles published in journals that advanced their careers.

I applied when I was a rising junior, but I didn't get in.

The leader that year was a woman, Professor Sandra Something.

She took one look at me, and it was a hard no. She could imagine the class discussions. Why are all the men so much nicer to Laura Lee? She was having none of it. She couldn't see writing a paper on the fact that young men want to impress a pretty girl.

———

I'd wanted to be a psychologist or psychiatrist ever since I was a little girl and I saw, on TV, a '60s black-and-white film, *The Three Faces of Eve*.

Joanne Woodward played a meek housewife with multiple personalities. Dissociative disorder, they call it now. One self is a very good girl, the other a very bad party girl who keeps trying to kill the good one's daughter, until a kindly doctor traces Eve's trauma back to her being forced to kiss her dead grandmother's corpse goodbye. As soon as the memory surfaces, a new, healthy personality named Jane emerges and gets rid of both the good and bad Eves forever.

I knew not to tell anyone how much I loved that film. Maybe it seemed creepy. When grown-ups asked what I wanted to do when I grew up, I said I wanted to help people be happier. Grown-ups loved that answer.

The truth was: I wanted to bring them back to that moment of kissing dead Grandma goodbye. I wanted to help them find out what had split them into pieces.

———

At the end of junior year, we applied to get into the class for the next fall. Everyone knew that the class would be way more over-subscribed than usual.

That year's facilitator was a star. A college legend.

Professor John James Randall was Professor Muller's favorite, most brilliant disciple. Though he was still in his thirties, Professor Randall already held an endowed chair in the department. It was understood that he would take over from Muller when—and if—the department head ever stepped down.

Professor Randall had been away for two years on a fellowship in Zurich. His absence had contributed to his stardom and the popularity of his class.

Of course I'd heard about him—how brilliant and charismatic he was—but I'd never seen him.

I was shaking when I knocked on his office door. Everyone said he was handsome, but nothing prepared me for the radiant movie star with his feet up on his desk. He was wearing cowboy boots so elaborately tooled and stitched that they might have looked silly on a less beautiful man. His hair was shiny, blue-black comic-book hair, lightly sprinkled with gray. His soft, generous mouth looked like a sea creature growing from the chiseled coral of his face.

He wore jeans and a black turtleneck sweater. Even in the no-toriously loose psych department, most professors wore shirts and ties. His retro aviator glasses (cool at the time) gave his eye sockets a slightly bruised tinge.

Without speaking or moving except to turn his head, he looked me up and down. Men could still do that then. It was a corny and sexist thing to do, everyone knew that. It made me feel as if I wasn't entirely myself, because the crazy thing was, I liked it.

It's not a feminist thing to say, but I am being honest: it was the most interesting thing that had happened at college.

He took off his glasses.

His eyes were smoky, intense, set deep in their sockets. His dark lashes were longer than mine.

"Look at you," he said.

Did any man ever say anything cornier? Or more offensive? I should have turned and left. Except that I was flattered.

"And you are?"

"Laura Lee?" Why did it sound like a question? How totally idiotic.

"Lorelei?"

"Laura Lee."

"That's wrong. All wrong. You do know that your parents gave you the wrong name, don't you? You should be Lorelei. You know who Lorelei was, I assume?"

Yes, I knew who the Lorelei was. I'd learned about her in high school when we studied the *Odyssey*. The Sirens. The Lorelei was the German Siren. She sang to you, and you lost your mind, and your ship smashed into a rock.

I knew, but I shook my head no. I wanted to hear him tell me.

"Condemned to death for bewitching men, she threw herself off a high rock along the Rhine. And all the sailors who sailed past had to stop up their ears, like Odysseus passing the Sirens. Because if they heard her song and saw her beauty, they'd crash into the shore and die. Is that who you are, Lorelei?"

Remembering this, twenty years later, I think, *What total bullshit!* Then why do I recall every word, *after twenty years*? Why didn't it sound like bullshit then?

I said, "The problem is, I can't sing." My little joke fell flat. I felt my face turn tomato red.

"Lorelei, I know when someone's lying. It's my professional training. Do you know what I think? I think you have a beautiful voice, don't you, Lorelei?"

"Busted." I smiled, stupidly. He was right. I could sing. In high school, when my friends and I went into Manhattan, we used to sing harmony in the subway stations because the acoustics were great.

"And *do* you have the power to lure men to their deaths?"

How did I not bursting out laughing?

"Why would I want to do something like that?" All right, we were flirting.

"Like what?" He was making me say it.

"Like lure men to their deaths." My whole body snapped from hot to cold and back to hot again. I just had to get the words out, and then it was his turn to speak.

"I'll bet you have the power. What's so attractive about you is that you don't know it."

He broke into a perfectly calibrated smile. Open, bright. He had gorgeous teeth. Looking at his face was like staring into a flashlight. Blinding. I looked away. At what? A big wooden desk, bookshelves, stacks of books and papers. Your basic faculty office. But on a hook behind the door hung a frayed and faded woman's terry cloth bathrobe, and on one of the shelves there was a coffee mug, tea bags, a hot plate, and a jar of powdered coffee creamer.

"This isn't my office," he said. "I'm camping out here. I just got back from two years in Switzerland. I'm still getting settled."

"I know," I said. "I mean . . . I heard you were away . . . I . . ."

"I'm in massive culture shock," he said. "Deep."

I didn't know what to say.

"Your application?" he said. "For the class?"

This was before we did everything by email. More physical paper changed hands then. I handed him my application file. One page, printed out.

He read as far as my address. "You live off campus?"

"I will. I'm going to. Next year. I have a cat. Pyewacket."

Why had I said that? Why did I think he needed to know about my cat?

"Pyewacket. The witch's familiar. Are you a witch in addition to being a siren, Lorelei?"

"No! I mean . . . no!" I couldn't believe he knew about Pyewacket's name!

"Then how did you come up with the name? Wait. Let me guess. *Bell, Book and Candle.*"

My favorite film! Kim Novak plays a beautiful witch from a family of witches. Despite herself, she falls in love with an ordinary human, Jimmy Stewart. And Pyewacket is her cat. The pretty witch's pretty feline familiar.

I was so shocked that he knew that, I grabbed onto the back of a chair because my knees were about to buckle.

"That's right," I said. "That's amazing. How did you know?"

He smiled and said nothing.

I babbled on, just to fill the silence. "That's my favorite movie. Anyway, pets aren't allowed in the dorms. He's a therapy cat. My doctor wrote a letter."

"Seriously?" Professor Randall was smiling at me so hard I thought his face must hurt. In memory, his smile is patronizing. Condescending. But I didn't think so then.

I thought, *What serious person leads with her kitty-cat's name?* I don't know why my cat was the most important thing about me. Maybe because I was closer to my cat than to another human being.

Until then, I hadn't made a lot of friends at college. I didn't know why. Social life confused me. People didn't seem to get my jokes, and I didn't get theirs. Guys seemed scared of me, even though I was pretty, or maybe *because* I was pretty. Maybe it would seem too obvious to choose a girl like me. Or maybe they already sensed something . . . off, something hidden inside me that would rise to the surface later.

The only "real" friend I made—Holly—I would meet in Professor Randall's class.

"I'm planning to live alone with my cat," I said.

"No boyfriend. No roommates? I mean . . . no *human* roommates?"

It sounded a little . . . personal, but this was the psych department. This was back in the day. Different times, different standards, different rules applied.

"Yes," I said. "Just us."

He smiled again. "Welcome to IP 121, Lorelei Green. That's how I'm listing you on the class roster, so inform the registrar. There's a waiting list, so please let the department know if your plans change. Otherwise, we'll see you in the fall."

We'll see you in the fall. He'd said *we*, not *I*. That proved that this had been a professional conversation. Not the flirtatious chat I'd imagined.

"Thank you thank you thank you."

"One thank-you is enough," he said.

"Okay. Then . . . just . . . thank you."

"That's four, Lorelei," he said.

That was how young I was: I let him change my name.

I changed my name for him, the first time we met.

I was Lorelei from then on.

———

When I went home that summer, I told my parents I wanted to be called Lorelei. My mother laughed. They refused.

My dad said, "In case we ever doubted that college is a big waste of money."

I went to the county courthouse and petitioned for a name change. I filled out all the papers. I got an amended birth certificate. I made duplicates of all the forms and left them on the kitchen table for my parents to find.

They didn't speak to me for a couple of weeks. Then they forgave me, sort of. But they never once called me Lorelei. They called me Laura Lee until they died. Hanging on to the name they chose. It was always all about *them*.

I told my cat, "I'm Lorelei now."

Pyewacket believed me.

Chapter Six

I'D FOUND Pyewacket the previous summer, in an outdoor drug market on the Lower East Side. He was just a kitten. I saved him from impaling himself on a discarded syringe he was rolling back and forth between his paws like a cat toy.

I didn't tell my (future) professor this. I didn't want him asking what I was doing in a weedy lot littered with drug paraphernalia. Though of course there was always a chance that he might think it was cool.

It wasn't cool. I'd gone there with a guy I was dating. Sort of dating.

The father of a patient in the pediatric practice where I worked as a receptionist during the summer.

Strep Throat Dad was a coke freak. That should have raised a red flag. He was rich enough to have his drugs hand-delivered to his office in Midtown or his home in Tribeca. But he didn't want his family finding out.

That scared him more than a drug market patrolled by jittery teenagers. Maybe he liked the double life: the wife and kids, the money, the street drugs. A triple life if you counted the abusive sex life he lived with me.

I think that the secrecy was what got him off. Some people are like that. Especially men.

I waited for Strep Throat Dad to find his dealer. It wasn't like any scene I knew, but I wasn't scared. It was a market. People were doing business. They weren't interested in me unless I had money, which I didn't. Unless I was a cop, which I wasn't. Or unless I was looking to buy drugs, which I also wasn't. I was with my boyfriend, who wasn't my boyfriend, just the father of my boss's patient.

He'd asked me out when he dropped by the office to pick up his son's antibiotics prescription.

In the drug market/vacant lot, I was so busy looking around that I almost tripped on something—something soft and furry. It yelped, and I did too. When I looked down, I saw a ginger-colored kitten. At least I thought it was ginger. Its fur was so dusty, so matted and streaked with grime, that it was hard to tell what color it was.

The kitten was playing with a syringe, rolling it back and forth.

I'd never had a pet. My parents hated animals.

I was a little afraid of the cat, even though he was a kitten. I guess that it was because of where we were and what he was doing. And because I knew nothing about cats. Something about that sweet stray kitten called out to me.

Destiny, I think now.

I picked up the kitten. God knows what he'd been rolling in. I buried my face in his soft, improbably sweet-smelling fur.

It was love at first sight. Mutual surrender.

A super-skinny white girl with matted, lime-green dreadlocks floated up to me. She leaned close. Too close. Her breath smelled like Jolly Ranchers and something acrid and stale.

"That's Pyewacket," she said.

"*Bell, Book and Candle*," I said. "That's the name of the cat in *Bell, Book and Candle*." This junkie girl and I both liked the same movie. The girl just looked at me. Bonding over a favorite movie wasn't one of her interests. "Anyway, that's what I call him. You could call him what you want. He was born here. His mom's dead, run over by a car. You should adopt him. He'll have a better life. I don't know where you live, but anywhere would be better than here. He's cute. He needs to be rescued. Look. He's *begging* you to save him."

"Okay," I said. "Pyewacket."

The name of the beautiful witch's beautiful cat. It was destiny, right?

After he bought the coke, Strep Throat Dad took me back to his duplex loft in Tribeca. His wife and kids were out in Montauk.

He gave Pyewacket a big dish of milk, which the thirsty, hungry kitten slurped up in a few seconds. It was nice of Strep Throat Dad, and I was glad to have a little while to think before I had to go home and deal with my parents and the fact that now we had a cat.

My "date" refilled the milk dish and brought it into the bedroom. Pyewacket followed, and so did I.

Strep Throat Dad put the milk dish on the floor, then he pushed me down on the bed—hard—and raped me.

I tried to float above my body, but I couldn't figure out where to go, and I was afraid to feel even more separated from myself. I remember thinking that if I left my body I might never get back in again. If I rose too far above this, my spirit would crash into the ceiling.

The worst thing was how little it had to do with me. The feeling that I didn't exist. The person who still called herself Laura Lee could have been a blow-up sex doll with arms, legs, a pelvis that was starting to ache, a mouth that was trying to scream except that a man's hand was covering it.

His palm tasted salty and gross. I shut my mouth. It was humiliating and disgusting.

It could have been worse. He wore a condom.

It could have been worse. He didn't hurt me.

It could have been worse. If not for him, I would never have found Pyewacket.

On my way home in the express bus, I cried into the kitten's soft fur.

Then a strange thing happened. The kitten got his back up, just a little. A shiver went through him, and he looked at me, looked deep into my eyes. I saw his face in the flashing lights shining through the bus window.

I knew that the cat was telling me that everything would be all right. He was promising me that my life was going to get better and that he would never leave me. He knew what had happened to me that night. He'd watched it happen, and now he had come to console me.

————

It was strange that my parents allowed me to keep Pyewacket. They were usually unaware of—indifferent to—how I felt, or when I'd been hurt, or whether I was happy or miserable. Like I said, they hated animals. But I think even they, cold as they were, sensed that I had been through something bad. They sensed that the cat might help.

"All right," my mother said. "But the minute you let him out of your room, I'm opening the front door, and you'll never see him again."

I didn't believe that Pyewacket would desert me just because my mother opened the door, but I kept him in my room with the door shut. He was happier there. He slept in my bed—on my chest. His purring put me to sleep all through that awful summer.

That summer, I went to my rapist's house and had sex with him every weekend. I couldn't believe I was doing it. Now they'd say it was trauma or shock, but no one talked that way then. The sex was nothing, just uncomfortable, a heavy guy lying on top of me so I could hardly breathe. It made me wonder why people made such a fuss about sex. The same question had occurred to me with my rough high-school-chess-champion boyfriend.

I don't know why I did it. I don't know what I expected. No one was forcing me really. It was something I was doing.

It nearly broke my heart to leave my cat with my parents all through my junior year of college. But Pyewacket wasn't allowed in the dorm, and, since I'd found him over the summer, I hadn't made arrangements. The reason I phoned home so often that semester was to make sure he hadn't escaped "by accident" when mom got tired of emptying his litter box. She'd thought she was finished with messes.

Jesus, Laura Lee. It stinks.

Lorelei. My name is Lorelei.

Why couldn't they understand?

At least I'd be able to live with my cat during my senior year.

Chapter Seven

I SPENT THE summer thinking about Professor Randall. He was like a destination, a place I went to when I was falling asleep. In my mind, it was already September, and I was already in school. The sweltering summer was already over.

My mom said I was never going to be a psychiatrist, or a therapist: I *needed* a psychiatrist. She said that she and my father should be spending their money on that instead of wasting it on my ridiculously expensive college. Considering the slutty way I dressed, I'd wind up with three kids by the time I was forty, and a husband cheating on me with his secretary.

Now when my mom said things like that, I felt like she was helping. Toughening me up. People said that Interpersonal Relations 121 could get ugly. If the other students ganged up on me, I would have had practice. I would be able to take it. My mom was preparing me for how it felt to be unfairly attacked.

When the rapist dad from the previous summer called, I was pleasant to him, but I said I couldn't see him. I said I was "seeing someone." I meant Professor Randall, though of course I was only "seeing" him in my imagination.

Strep Throat Dad laughed.

He said, "You're seeing someone, Laura Lee? I'm married. Remember?"

"That's Lorelei. I can't remember anything," I said. And I hung up.

I said *seeing*. I meant I'd *seen* the teacher—the facilitator—whose class I'd be taking in the fall. Already he had saved me from another summer of self-destructive behavior.

Do things happen for a reason? Some things do. If I hadn't gone out with my rapist, I wouldn't have found Pyewacket. If it wasn't for Pyewacket, I might not have moved off campus. If I hadn't lived off campus . . .

If I hadn't. If I hadn't.

———

You already know that this part of the story is not going to end well. But you can only judge me if you have never once in your life done something stupid because of a crush on a powerful and charismatic older person.

All that summer, I went over my brief conversation with Professor Randall until I'd wrung it dry. I'd exhausted the possibilities that our little talk gave me. After that, I needed to imagine things that hadn't happened.

Yet.

I imagined him showing up at my apartment door. A little shy. Blushing, maybe.

It's fine, I would say. I'm glad you're here. *I knew you would come. I couldn't stop thinking about you.*

———

Student-faculty sex was already frowned upon, but it still happened, a lot. The situation wasn't the same as now. Teachers weren't fired for sleeping with students. Especially not a professor in the Woodward psych department. Especially not Professor Muller's protégé.

I couldn't forget how Professor Randall had looked at me. All that summer, I hoped and prayed for him to look at me that way again.

I'd gotten last summer's job back, filling in as a receptionist for Dr. Steiner, my kindly former pediatrician, whose wife usually worked the front office. Since I was his patient, he'd moved his practice to Manhattan, and I commuted in by train to work for him.

During the summer his kids were home from school, so I did Mrs. Steiner's job, which was easy. Making appointments, answering the phone, triaging the genuine emergencies from the spoiled rich moms trying to jump the line.

Thinking about my professor-to-be, I was distracted at work. I got appointments mixed up. I filed charts in the wrong order.

One of the many things I still hold against Professor Randall is that he made me waste an entire summer in the prime of my life.

Thinking back, that was the last summer when I was . . . okay. When I still looked forward to the future.

I liked living in my childhood bedroom with my cat, who made it a different place. A place where someone loved me.

In the evenings when I came home from work, I'd pick up Pyewacket and feel a shudder of joy going through him straight to my pleasure center. All night Pyewacket snuggled under my chin, and I had the feeling that we were dreaming the same dreams.

———

Senior year I left for school a week early to set up my new apartment. It was on the third floor of a three-decker wooden house in Great Barrington. Living there was cheaper than living in the dorm. My parents liked that part. My mother called it a fire trap, but she didn't seem worried about me burning up.

My parents liked that my landlady, Mrs. O'Neal, lived on the first floor. She sat by her window day and night. She told my parents, who had to co-sign the lease for me, that she was renting me the apartment—she didn't usually rent to undergrads—because my parents had a clean car. They liked the sound of that. Maybe they were flattered and didn't ask themselves what the cleanliness of their car had to do with anything.

They came with me to buy furniture from the Goodwill. Dad severely undertipped the guys who dragged it up three stories. As soon as they drove away, Mrs. O'Neal told me, "I don't meddle in my tenants' business as long as they're not noisy and don't do anything dangerous and take out the garbage so we don't get bugs."

I was relieved to hear that. If someone—let's say, a man; let's say, a professor—came to visit, she wouldn't complain or call my parents.

Pyewacket wasn't a problem for Mrs. O'Neal. She herself had three cats. Her apartment smelled like a cat box. I was glad that mine didn't. The tenants had left it sweet and spotless.

Pyewacket and I had everything. The apartment was our kingdom. I was happy, or almost. I lay on my bed, watching the ceiling fan. A summer breeze blew in the window through the ivy. I was looking forward to school. I was nervous, but excited.

I remember feeling that the coming year would change my life.

Chapter Eight

ON THE first day of a normal class, the students check one another out, and pretend not to. But in IP 121 we were *meant* to look around and see what we could figure out about our fellow students. To remember and record our first impressions.

It wasn't a normal classroom. It was more like I imagined an airport business-class lounge, only without the bar and snacks. Armchairs were arranged in a circle, each with a little desk, like the folding tables on which my parents ate dinner in front of the TV.

We were supposed to take notes. My notebook must have disappeared during the years between then and now. I wish I had it now.

I still have a few paperback books from college—a copy of Beckett, *Totem and Taboo*, *Macbeth*. I hardly recognize the clear, stiff little-girl printing in which I wrote my dopey marginal scribbling:

First sign of ambition? Symbol of hopelessness? I agree!

Ten of us—three women, seven men—sat in a semicircle. Professor Randall sat just outside the circle, with an empty space in front of him so he could watch us all pretending that we weren't jumping out of our skins.

I wish I had one of those class pictures—like the ones they take in grade school—to remind me of who was in the group. I remember the women. There were only three. Me and Holly and a preppy girl who never said much.

A girl I hardly remember except for her name.

Miranda DeWitt.

A name I would later borrow for my Woman of the Year dinner guest. The real Miranda had died young, in a skiing accident at Davos. So I didn't think she'd mind if I tried to imagine what she would have become if she'd lived. A divorcing Park Avenue wife. I went to the gala dinner as the person she might have been.

A living memorial, you could say.

———

So who *was* in that class? Interpersonal Relations 121.

Me.

A tall girl with gap teeth and freckles who turned out to be Holly.

Miranda DeWitt, who stared into the middle distance and acted like it was causing her mortal pain to say one word.

A guy from the Midwest, Drew, who mentioned how much he liked girls and how much girls liked him. Holly snickered, and the class turned on her, everyone but me. Everyone turning against you was something you had to watch out for. No one wanted it to happen to them.

It happened a lot that semester. Someone would say something, and everyone would pounce on a lie or an exaggeration or an unfair passive-aggressive attack.

It was like spin the bottle, except that when it landed on you, you didn't get kissed. You got to be told, by the group, what a bad person you were.

There was one nice guy—I'm pretty sure his name was Mark—whose dad wrote bestsellers, and Joel Something von Something, who later wrote a popular book about psychopharmacology and hallucinogenic plants. They were neutral presences. One guy, Tim, wore a trench coat and acted like the NPR foreign correspondent he later became.

Another of the guys, Mitch Berger, went on to be a TV reporter. What are the odds of that? I still see him every so often on the local news, though not on the national network or the foreign capitals he probably hoped to be sent to. Mostly they have him on Long Island, covering stormy weather and traffic accidents. There was also a guy named Ted, the star of our loser lacrosse team, who picked fights with everyone and by the end was the one everyone picked on. He became a successful brain surgeon.

There was one more boy I can't remember. Probably he became a psychiatrist or therapist, which is why you went to Woodward.

Holly was the only one whose career I followed closely.

Even though I never graduated, even though I dropped out before the second semester of senior year and am not even an official alumna, even though I am the girl least likely to cough up the big bucks, Woodward College has kept me in its sights. It's tracked me to my apartment with hilarious appeals for donations and their glossy alumni magazine featuring attractive new faculty members, superstar recent graduates, tepid classmate gossip, accounts of retirements and deaths.

I look at the cover. I riffle through it, looking for information about anyone I used to know.

Then I throw it in the trash.

———

Holly was the one who became my friend. The one I thought was my friend.

She was the first real friend I made at school. The joy of making a new friend erased all the loneliness I'd experienced during my first three years at college.

Our childhoods were similar in many ways. She was raised by a single mom in eastern Iowa, I'd grown up on Long Island, but we'd both suffered from . . . let's call it a lack of love. We traded stories about our high school experiences. Her football star boyfriend had been as sexually inept as my clumsy chess champion. She'd been just as lonely, just as sad.

I even told her about the rapist dad who'd taken me to the street drug market. We talked about Professor Randall, about how handsome he was. The one thing I didn't tell her about was the flirty vibe I'd gotten from him in his office the previous spring. I'm not sure why I kept that secret. Maybe the future was whispering a warning.

For the first time, someone understood. I'd met someone I could trust.

Wrong again.

Our classmates were fodder for Holly and me, for our forbidden gossip. Forbidden, because we weren't supposed to talk about the class outside of class. Not even—especially!—with fellow students. Naturally, that meant that Holly and I couldn't talk about anything else.

Until we stopped talking.

———

That first day, we all stared at our hands, or pretended to look up something in our notebooks. Professor Randall watched us pretend, and we pretended we didn't notice him watching.

Professor Randall didn't seem to remember that he and I had met. He didn't remember he'd looked me up and down or that our conversation had grown . . . flirtatious. When he read my name—Lorelei Green—off the attendance sheet, he gave no sign of recalling that he'd changed it. That he'd renamed me. And that I'd let him.

If he was pretending to forget, he was a very good actor. Or maybe he really had forgotten that I used to be Laura Lee. That should have been a warning: the conversation that changed me forever hardly registered with him.

But what could he have said? How would he have signaled that he thought I was special?

No one spoke for a long time. The room was pin-drop quiet (that was how the real estate listing had described my apartment!) except that, every few minutes, Professor Randall made a funny sound, a little snort, a momentary exhale. I didn't remember him doing that last spring when we met in his office. Was it something he only did in class? Or something that had started over the summer? Did he have allergies? A sinus problem?

The silence seemed possibly endless. We'd heard that the facilitator wouldn't speak until one of us spoke first. We were prepared to wait it out. But how long could the wait last?

Professor Randall stared ahead, unfocused. He looked as if he was thinking deeply about . . . what? As if he had a lot on his mind. From time to time he made that soft little snort: a sound I imagined a deer making on a summer night in the forest.

I remember who broke that first silence. Mitch, the one who became a reporter. He said he had a confession.

A confession already! We hadn't even started.

He was on the staff of the student newspaper. He'd been assigned to write a series called "Inside IP 121." He wanted to make sure everyone was on board with him writing about us. Was he boasting about his assignment or asking our permission?

He *was* asking permission. But not ours. He was asking our professor.

"An exposé?" Professor Randall said. "You're writing an exposé? Telling all our dirty little secrets?"

"Not necessarily. Well, okay, maybe a little."

Professor Randall shot Mitch a look that wiped the fake-embarrassed, pleased-with-himself smile right off his face.

"It is decidedly *not* okay. How will we trust one another without the assumption of privacy that everything depends on? Everything that happens here, everything that matters. You will either have to drop the class or sign a statement that you can get from the department secretary. A legally binding promise not to write about the class. And you need to have it notarized."

"But, Professor, what about my First Amendment rights?"

Professor Randall shrugged. "Oh, please. I'm not suggesting that you can't write the piece. I'm saying you can't be in the class if you plan to write about it. I assume you know there's a waiting list. The class is way oversubscribed. It won't be hard to fill your place with a student who can follow our fairly simple, straightforward rules. You don't write about our class. You don't even talk about our class, though I know that no one follows that one."

There was some nervous fake laughter. Professor Randall gave the ones who'd laughed a look: he knew it was nervous and fake. I was glad I hadn't laughed. I was relieved and disappointed that he didn't look at me. Not once. It was exciting and frustrating. I felt an unfamiliar tension jittering through my body.

I loved how he talked. His tone, his word choice. His delicate sarcasm. Everything about him. Even that funny little snort.

"Okay," said Mitch. "Sorry. I won't write about the class. I promise. I'll sign the pledge."

———

I didn't think that the first class was supposed to begin with a tense exchange between the professor and the boy reporter. But now it gave the other guys something to do. Mitch's apology hadn't satisfied them. In fact, it set them off. They took turns insulting him for trying to pimp out our education to advance his pitiful career at the student paper. The most aggressive said that Mitch's ambition was gross, as if we all weren't ambitious, as if that wasn't how we'd gotten there. We were just better at hiding our ambition, which made Mitch the Piggy in our *Lord of the Flies*. I had the feeling these guys weren't so nasty outside of class. They believed it was expected of them, or permitted, or encouraged.

The three women said nothing in that first class, or several classes after. We watched. I remember feeling anxious. Butterflies in my stomach and chest.

While everyone was looking at Mitch and his tormentors, I finally felt free to take a good look at Professor Randall. He was as handsome as I remembered, except that in his office he'd smiled at me, and now his face was as cold and still as granite. He was watching and taking notes. Watching and taking notes. He wasn't aware of me. I had wasted months dreaming about him. I had wasted a summer that I would never get back.

One of the guys said it first, and then the others agreed that Mitch was narcissistic. They were probably all psych majors. Performing for our teacher. Though I guess we were all playacting, in a way. I was performing shyness.

The guys looked at Professor Randall to confirm their diagnosis. But he wasn't taking the bait. He would talk when he wanted to talk. Or never. He had mystery and depth, or anyway, mystery, which you could choose to see as depth.

I chose to see it as depth.

A confession: whenever I hear about saints and spiritual and political leaders, I think of him. Not long ago I watched a documentary in which a cult member described her guru as having an aura like the ring of light around a streetlamp on a rainy night. "You could see it," she'd said. "We all could."

I saw the light around our professor.

A couple of the guys would have been happy to insult Mitch for the entire semester. But after two more classes, Holly spoke up:

"Can I say something? None of the women in this class have said one word since we introduced ourselves that first day. We're not interested in quarreling with Mitch, so we feel left out."

Even then, I guess, she was in training to be the Woman of the Year.

That shut them up. Maybe Holly was *already* Woman of the Year, except that she was still Holly Snopes, not Holly Serpenta. And no one paid any special attention to her.

Yet.

———

Our first in-class assignment was to make two-minute sketches of the other students. Professor Randall gave out paper and charcoal.

It was a weird experiment, everyone staring at everyone else, one by one, then moving on to the next person, drawing, turning pages, knowing we were all probably being stared at by grad students and junior faculty sitting behind the one-way glass. It was like speed dating on steroids and in hell.

We were on a timer. Two minutes, *bing!* You moved on. It was extremely intense, staring at someone drawing you so that you could draw them.

We were told to make each sketch on a separate piece of paper. When everyone was finished, we were instructed to give our drawings to the people we'd drawn. Then we were supposed to look at them and say how we felt about how the others had portrayed us.

Some of the drawings were pretty skillful. Some looked as if a first grader had done them. Woodward was not an art school.

When it was my turn, I said, "All the men in the class drew me with way bigger breasts than I have."

The men got quiet. Professor Randall snorted twice. Miranda De-Witt looked at me for the first and last time. Holly burst out laughing.

It wasn't a fake laugh. It was real. That was when I knew that we were going to be friends.

I wondered if she noticed that our teacher was finally looking at me.

Looking at my breasts.

I suppose he had a good reason: he was comparing them with the sketches.

After class I invited Holly over to have tea and meet Pyewacket.

Chapter Nine

THE WOMAN of the Year has outgrown or erased Holly's freckles and lost thirty pounds. Her wide face is narrow, her skin taut, her bone structure perfect. She doesn't even have the same smile. It's a doll smile, a puppet smile. The gap between her front teeth has disappeared.

I envy her cosmetic dentist.

———

I had a crush on my professor, but I was in love with my cat. I've had other cats since, but it was never the same. Maybe it was first love. Maybe Pyewacket was all I ever wanted. A creature who loved me. Whom I could depend on.

At last.

People who say, "A dog will lick your face, but a cat will show you its tail" . . . they don't know cats. Every time Pyewacket heard my key in the door he trotted over and rubbed against my leg. I have never been happier to see another living creature. I grabbed him and snuggled him and put him down, and he stepped back and watched me take off my coat. He waited politely outside the bathroom door, then followed me into the kitchen. He watched me pour a bowl of milk for him, a glass of wine for me. Chin chin, salud, we've made it through another day. Another glass for me, then—usually—another.

I guess I was already drinking a little too much in college. But everybody was, so it was as if no one noticed. Or no one cared. As if it didn't matter.

Pyewacket woke me at exactly seven every morning. Anyone who knows cats will tell you that they have a very clear, very precise sense of time.

Did I say he was a ginger cat? They call redheads gingers, but that's wrong. Redheads aren't ginger-colored, and neither was Pyewacket. He was a lovely pale orange with patches of white and a silvery aura. Black marks, like drawn-on whiskers, ran under his actual whiskers. He had a highly intelligent face. People who say that cats don't have the full range of human expressions also don't know cats.

He sat at my feet when I ate, sat next to me when I read or worked at my desk. He kept my toes warm in bed. He knew when I wanted or didn't want to be cuddled and touched. We communicated so perfectly, it was a joke that we belonged to different species. I knew he never forgot that I had saved him from a lot littered with medical waste, but that wasn't a big deal for us. It wasn't our defining moment. It was just something that happened.

I depended on him for so much. For company and affection. And as a judge of character. He'd been wary of my parents, though they were reasonably nice to him. Tolerant, at least. Still, he saw them for who they were. Unpredictable. Cold. Unloving. Not to be trusted.

He liked Holly right away. He purred hello, and she picked him up, and they snuggled for a while. I wasn't even jealous. I was thrilled that they got along.

I asked Holly if she had cats, and she said that her mother had never let her have a pet, which was something else we had in common. My mother had only agreed when I told her where I found Pyewacket—and she sensed that something terrible had happened to me. She couldn't have known about the rape, but what minimal maternal instincts she had must have kicked in and told her something. Her hard heart softened, or maybe she was afraid that if she said no, I'd tell her what I was doing in the lot and what happened to me afterward. Some mothers want you to tell them everything, and some mothers—mine—prefer you to tell them nothing.

Did I imagine that my cat was a person? I knew that my cat was a cat. If I'd thought he was a person, I wouldn't have loved him as much.

The big lie was pretending to like people as much as I liked my cat.

Holly and I talked about our shared desire to become therapists or psychiatrists. That's why we'd come to Woodward. We agreed that our loveless childhoods had made us more vulnerable. More empathetic.

You might think, with my passions and priorities, that I might have wanted to be a veterinarian. But I like animals too much for that. I couldn't have brought myself to hurt them, even if it meant making them well.

Chapter Ten

WHAT WOULD my Woman of the Year tablemates think if I announced that there were months when the Woman of the Year and I spent hours every day sprawled across my bed, in my shabby student apartment, talking our heads off?

Pyewacket would watch us from the floor. Sometimes he jumped up on the bed. I knew that he understood what we were saying. I was so glad that Holly wasn't allergic to cats.

Nut allergies are better in every way. Certainly for my purposes—I mean, for the purpose that brought me to the gala dinner. Few people go into shock from cat allergies. They just wheeze and sneeze a lot.

A nut allergy could lay you out. That was why I was there.

I got up and stood on my toes so that I could see the Woman of the Year. I had never in my life been so invested in someone eating her salad. Though Holly couldn't see me, I attacked my own salad like a parent encouraging a child to eat, by example. *Eat! Eat! Look at me! Eat!*

———

I knew from the start that sooner or later the students in Interpersonal Relations 121 would come after me. I tried to be friendly and pleasant and not make enemies. I didn't mention how much I was drinking. I complained about my other classes. I did an imitation of my landlady, Mrs. O'Neal, sitting at her window and staring out at the street.

The other students criticized me for that. They said I was being ageist and snobbish. I agreed and said I was sorry. I remember Mitch saying that he had the feeling that the men in the class were competing for my approval, though they would never admit it.

Maybe that caused the first rift in my friendship with Holly. Was she insulted that no one suggested that the boys were performing for *her*? Was she jealous? We pretended that we were above jealousy. That the power of our friendship exempted us from female competition.

Years ago I was the obvious winner of that unacknowledged contest. Now she'd won. And she'd turned into someone else: the entire world was jealous of her, and she was jealous of no one.

Flash forward twenty years. and everyone was performing for *her*: Gloria Steinem and a half dozen women she'd rescued—women whose lives she'd saved.

———

Professor Randall hardly ever said anything except at the very end of class. Then he'd say, "See you next time, same time, same place," and he'd make that funny little snort.

So it was a little startling when, after Mitch suggested that the guys were competing for my attention, our professor finally spoke up. "Lorelei, do *you* feel that these guys are performing for you?"

I thought about it a moment.

I said, "I wouldn't know."

Sometimes I felt a connection with him even though we hardly looked at each other and barely exchanged two consecutive words.

Even so, by the third week of class, I sensed that something was happening. Something was starting up. Something that could not be mentioned, and maybe never would, though I thought about him nonstop, just as I had since we'd met. Other times, I told myself that our special connection was all in my imagination. Wishful thinking.

Outside of class, Holly and I laughed about a classmate who had just been busted for having two girlfriends, one at Clark and one at UMass Amherst. We imitated Miranda DeWitt staring into space and smiling blankly when someone asked why she didn't speak, then answering that she didn't have to, before gazing off into the distance again.

Holly did great imitations. She could imitate everyone in the class.

Playing the part of Holly Serpenta—Italian aristocrat by marriage, do-gooder, Woman of the Year—probably came naturally to her. Or almost. She must have learned from the women in her first husband's Tuscan family. She began by watching, listening, imitating. Then she reinvented herself and turned smart, plain-looking Holly Snopes into the brilliant, beautiful Holly Serpenta.

———

One afternoon Holly—still Holly Snopes then—jumped up from my bed and flopped into a chair, crossed and uncrossed her legs. She was silent for a long time, pretending to take notes in an imaginary notebook, then snorted out her nose and said, "Who am I? Guess."

I picked up my cat and buried my face in his soft, warm fur. Pyewacket purred.

"That's too easy," I said.

———

My romantic dreams never got any further than the doorway, where in my imagination Professor Randall kept showing up. He'd apologize for bothering me, and I'd confess that I'd been thinking about him constantly since last spring.

My fantasy always ended there. I didn't know where else to take it.

Chapter Eleven

THE FIRST night he *did* show up felt like an extension of my dream, like one of those dreams in which you dream that you wake up. But you're still dreaming.

In my imagination, he was always just *there*. In reality, Mrs. O'Neal telephoned me and said a man was outside, at the door. He wanted to see me.

"A gentleman in cowboy boots."

I said, "Send him up."

I went to the window. Professor Randall was looking up at the building. We saw each other through the glass. His long shadow striped the sidewalk. It was really him. Why was he here?

It was a cold, raw early October evening, but I opened the windows and fanned the air. In my dream of his coming here, my apartment didn't smell like packaged ramen noodles.

He knocked. I opened the door.

He stood in the hallway, smiling, not even slightly winded

from the two steep flights. When my parents had helped me move in, they'd been breathless every time they came up.

"Come in." I made way for him to pass me.

As he looked around my apartment, I realized that I had decorated it in the hopes that my dream might come true. After my parents left, I'd put an orange shawl over the lamp, which cast a pumpkin-colored light on the ceiling. I'd bought an art deco poster advertising a theatrical performance in Paris in the 1920s, and a reproduction of Van Gogh's last sad painting of the crows skimming over the field.

He seemed to approve of what he saw. Or at least he didn't disapprove. I was too shy to ask him to sit down, so we continued to stand in the center of my little living room.

He said, "I met your very nice neighbor."

I could tell that he was nervous, too.

"Mrs. O'Neal," I repeated. "My landlady."

It was good to have something to talk about other than why he was there.

"In France she'd be called a concierge," he said.

This was how young I was: that he knew what Mrs. O'Neal would be called in France seemed crazily romantic. Irresistible, really! Also there was this: he'd just said more words than he'd said at any one time in an average class.

He couldn't look me in the eye. I couldn't look at him.

That alone was exciting.

He'd brought something for us to look at. To focus on.

A flower. A single flower.

It was a tulip, an intensely deep-red flower, with jagged black streaks like lightning bolts in the center of each fringed petal.

"A vampire tulip," he said. "That's what the breed is called. It's very beautiful, isn't it? I thought you'd like it. I brought it for you."

My professor was bringing me flowers. A flower. What could that possibly mean except . . . ?

I looked at the flower. I couldn't speak. I opened my mouth. I gulped the air like a fish.

A vampire tulip. Obviously. The color of blood. Not the bright blood that stains the paper towel when you've cut your finger, but the deep, dark blood that fills the tube when they take your blood at the lab.

He had a beautiful laugh. He never laughed in class. He had laughed in his office last spring. He'd saved his laughter for me.

"A vampire?" I said weakly. He'd already suggested I be named after a spirit who lured men to their deaths. Now was he saying that I sucked men's blood?

"Lorelei, I'm not suggesting we're vampires. I'm just saying it's beautiful, and it made me think of you."

Lorelei. The blood-colored tulip? Is that how he saw Laura Lee, the former high school cheerleader? I didn't ask where one would get such a flower in the fall, in a small college town in Western Massachusetts. I wouldn't have known how to ask.

"You do know what I mean, don't you, Lorelei?"

"Yes," I lied. I sank into a chair. He sat on the sofa opposite me.

I stared at the astonishing flower, which seemed to be opening in real time. I felt as if I were on some psychoactive drug. Or how I imagined that felt. I didn't do drugs, not even weed. I didn't like what they did to my head. I felt like I did when I went beyond my customary two—well, sometimes four—glasses of wine.

The point was: I didn't feel like . . . me. Like my normal self. Another warning sounded—*gong!*—but I chose not to listen.

I said, "Would you like some . . . ?" I didn't know what to offer him. Ramen noodles?

It's amazing how much I remember, twenty years later.

He said, "I'll have whatever you're having," and we laughed. Awk-ward!

That seemed like a strange way to start off a teacher-student visit.

"Professor Randall . . ." What a ridiculous thing to call a guy handing me a beautiful deep-red tulip that, he said, reminded him of me. What was I supposed to call him?

"Dell." He read my mind. "Call me Dell. My friends call me Dell."

As far as I could tell, no one in our class knew that simple fact about him. I was the only one. His friends? Was I his friend? How had we skipped all the steps from student and teacher to friends, and how many more were we going to skip on our way to . . . what?

We both knew what. There was no point pretending.

Professor Randall—Dell—reached down and scooped up Pyewacket, who'd been nuzzling his leg. He pressed him to one side of his long, handsome face. He'd shaved, and his skin looked very smooth, not that my cat would have cared. Blissed-out Pyewacket closed his eyes. They stayed liked that for a while. I had never seen anything sexier. Do I sound like a crazy person when I say that the sight of my teacher making out with my cat gave me a fluttery feeling in the pit of my stomach?

As I've said, Pyewacket was an excellent judge of character. Or so I thought at the time.

"This must be Pyewacket," Professor Randall said. I was having trouble thinking of him as Dell. It was going to take practice.

I was astonished that he remembered after almost six months.

That was the last time I'd mentioned Pyewacket. It took me a beat to recover. "You remembered from last spring?"

"Last spring? You talked about him in class."

Right. There had been a class in which everyone was supposed to say what we loved most. A few students mentioned their moms. Holly said her little brother. A few said their dogs. I said my cat. Pyewacket. Several guys smiled at me. A cute name for a cute girl's cat.

Professor Randall—Dell—broke his customary silence. "Can I tell you what I heard?"

Sure. He was the teacher. The leader. Facilitator, whatever. He could say what he wanted. Why was he even asking? And what had he heard?

He said, "None of the students mentioned a lover. Do young people no longer fall in love?"

I'd thought I would die when he said that. I'd thought I would die of love.

"What about you, Professor?" Mitch had asked. No one could believe his nerve.

Our professor's face had been a mask of nothing. "We're not here to talk about me."

Now, watching him nuzzle my cat, I thought, *I need to concentrate!* Concentrate? I couldn't think. The fantasy had come true. The same person but not the same. Not the same person in the dream, not the same man who taught our class.

Friendlier. More open. Warmer. More amused.

This person's name was Dell.

I don't know how I found the nerve to say, "Is this about class?" I knew it wasn't, but I had to ask.

"No," he said. "We're off the clock. Come over here, okay?"

Chapter Twelve

SINCE THEN I've had sex with twenty-three men, and I think that I probably won't ever have sex again. It's not that I'm too old. Not that I couldn't find someone if I wanted to. I just don't think it will happen. I don't want it. I don't want the trouble.

After Dell, each time I slept with another man, I thought of how you always hear that junkies are forever trying to get back to the rush of that first high.

Dell was that first rush.

After Dell, none of those other men registered. Would sex with Dell have been better or worse if I'd known that it would never feel that good again? It couldn't have been better.

It was nothing like being with the rapist Strep Throat Dad. Nothing like getting pounded by my clueless chess champion boyfriend.

I never felt pressured or out of control. Or maybe I felt a little out of control, but in a good way, like body surfing when you let yourself be carried by a wave. There's something swoony about the high of saying, or even thinking, *Do what you want*, and knowing that it would be exactly what I wanted. He kept asking, "Are you sure, Lorelei? Are you sure you want to do this?" He made asking sexy. He also made it consensual in case (I realized later) things ever came to that.

How could I answer? I could hardly breathe. Yes, I was sure I wanted to do this. But it wasn't *informed consent*. I was out of my mind. Not being able to say no was a symptom of illness.

The Strep Throat Dad rapist didn't ask if I was sure. My high school chess champion boyfriend never asked if I was sure. No one had ever asked.

I was surprised, really surprised, that this was so different. I was so sure.

When Dell came, he made that funny little snort.

How could I hear him make that noise in class without thinking about him making it in bed?

I thought, *My life is about to change.*

———

Dell loved Pyewacket, and Pyewacket loved him. Dell would reach down, and my cat would leap into his arms. He'd bring little treats—cans of gourmet tuna fish, a rubber mouse, a ribbon with a bell. As Pyewacket rolled the bell on the floor, delighted by the noise, I thought of how I'd saved him from playing with the syringe. I connected it with Dell being here. Both experiences were about rescue, though I couldn't have said what Dell was rescuing me from.

Every so often, Dell brought me one of those beautiful blood-red tulips. I bought a perfect small crystal vase at a yard sale, and it became a ceremony, putting the flower in water when both of us were so turned on that our knees were shaking.

Maybe it seems a little silly now, but it was deadly serious then.

He never did those creepy controlling things that older men do with younger women. He never told me what to wear or what music to like or what friends I could see. My only friend was Holly, and Dell and I both knew, without our having to say so, that I could never tell her.

I certainly wasn't going to talk about it in class.

After we started sleeping together, the class seemed entirely different. Sometimes I felt a little crazy, not looking at him, not thinking about what he did while I pretended to be interested when Holly tried to get Miranda DeWitt to tell the class what she'd been feeling.

I knew that Holly was semi-mad at me, though she pretended nothing was wrong. She knew that something was up. I'd changed. We hung out less often. She knew I was holding something back. She was taking it out on Miranda DeWitt, and it was hard not looking at Dell to see if he thought so too.

He was good at his job, and his job was staying out of it. Watching. Taking notes. His face was as sharp and still as the statues on Easter Island.

And yet . . . we had a secret.

Sometimes I looked at the one-way mirror and wondered if those presences on the other side of the looking glass suspected what was going on. If they picked up on something that my classmates—I hoped—couldn't see.

I talked in class, more than I did before, maybe because I was nervous, maybe because he was watching me and thinking about what we were doing. Or was he? Maybe I needed to prove to the class that nothing was going on, that I was a normal hardworking student. I forgot what I said as soon as I said it. I sometimes had to work to remember what I'd been talking about.

Maybe he was better at compartmentalizing. Maybe he wasn't thinking about me. He was working. Facilitating. Taking notes. Watching and saying nothing.

———

I never knew when he would show up at my apartment, so I stayed home waiting. He never spent the night. We never discussed it. Neither of us wanted him to sleep over. Mrs. O'Neal would have noticed. She wouldn't have liked it. She'd rather have kept on believing that her good-student tenant was being tutored by her professor.

He wasn't married. He didn't have kids. He'd had a serious girlfriend, but she'd gotten a job at Stanford, and they'd parted amicably. It was better for them both. How grown-up was that?

That was the sum total of what I knew about his personal life. His short bio on the college website mentioned a few published articles, all of them behind paywalls I couldn't afford to breach.

Any normal person would have tried to find out if Professor Randall had a history of sleeping with students. He was known for not even hanging around. Other professors—the charismatic ones—had acolytes who followed them like sucker fish trailing a shark. Their students went out drinking and went to dinner with them, babysat their kids, picked up their dry cleaning. Mostly those were the younger teachers, who were not all that much older than their students.

Professor Muller was one of the rare department heads who hung out with his students. Not in bars, of course. He and his wife gave dinner parties for new hires, junior faculty, and selected graduate students. Undergraduates weren't invited, but they could edge into his outer orbit by taking work-study jobs in his lab.

Professor Randall—Dell—was often a favored guest at Professor Muller's dinners, sitting at the table at the department chair's right hand. He was at the center—or anyway, near the center—of that charmed circle.

That he'd spent the last two years in Europe increased the mystery around him. No one knew what his life had been like in Zurich. Had there been beautiful Swiss girls? Young women who spoke five languages?

I didn't want to know. I didn't want to find out that I wasn't the only one, that I wasn't the first student he'd slept with, that I wasn't special. That he had a pattern, an ongoing story, and I was the latest installment.

I couldn't ask Holly. It was the one thing I couldn't tell her. It took effort to make it seem as if nothing had changed.

Dell and I were turning out to be good at keeping a secret. Sometimes I imagined that he and I could work as a research team. We could have one of those science marriages, like Pierre and Marie Curie.

Go ahead and judge me, you who have never been young.

———

Does the Woman of the Year remember that part of the story? Does she remember the guilty tone that crept into my voice when she and I gossiped about the psych class we were taking together?

She remembers a different story. The story she told the world.

Dell was the one I should have poisoned. But he was already dead.

———

DISGRACED PSYCHOLOGIST DIES IN FALL.

According to the story that appeared on the internet, former professor John James Randall, best known as Holly Serpenta's abuser, died in Mexico. He'd gone hiking and, it was assumed, fallen off a cliff into a deep ravine. Mudslides and bad weather had hampered the search and rescue operation. Though the operation had continued for a week, it was unsuccessful.

I wondered if anyone else had thought it was suicide. I did. His life had been ruined, his career destroyed. He'd lost his job, his home, his professional reputation. He'd been forced to leave his country because (the papers implied) he had no job, and life was cheaper south of the border.

But when there is no corpse, you can't help thinking . . . is the person really dead? Sometimes I'd imagine how, one day, he'd turn up at my doorstep and explain everything. He'd tell me that there had been a huge mistake, that what he'd done to me had been Holly's idea, and that he'd always loved me. He'd never stopped loving me.

Was that something I hoped for? Or was it something I feared?

———

I've said that he never told me what to read, but that wasn't entirely true. There were evenings when our pillow talk got a little . . . educational. I'd already read Freud in Intro to Psych, but he got me to read more. He was even more emphatic than Professor Muller in critiquing Freud's "worthless" and "deluded" ideas. We talked about it. In bed.

When we hashed over Freud's case study of the patient he called Dora, I remarked that Dora's father sold her to his business partner. Dell kissed me and said it wasn't just my beauty and my body but my brain he admired. Can you imagine how that felt? *Admired*, he said. Not *loved*. *Admired* was enough. When we read *The Wolf Man*, I said that the Wolf Man's problem was that insanity ran in his family and not that he'd seen his parents having sex. Dell went down on me for being such a genius.

When I try to remember how young I was, I think about the fact that I found it sexy to be in bed with a guy twenty years my senior, talking about Freud's case studies of traumatized girls. All these years later it seems funny, a little, even to me.

The serious pain, the lasting pain, was never about Dell.

That was the big surprise.

This is not a *love triangle story*, if that's what you are thinking.

———

Mostly we stayed inside, in my apartment, in bed. Sometimes Pyewacket curled up at our feet. I was happy that my lover (I had a lover!) and my cat got along so well. It made everything easier. I was curious to know if Pyewacket wondered what the humans were doing, or why he was seeing so much of Dell and so much less of his other friend, Holly.

One night, Dell said there was somewhere he had to go. He asked me to come with him.

Where?

School.

Why?

He had to do something.

Do what?

Something he did every few days.

He said, "Trust me."

I would have agreed even if he'd asked me to go watch him grade student papers.

Trust me, he'd said.

I trusted him.

He said, "There's something I want to show you."

What?

The psych labs.

We all knew what went on in those labs. They were the lowest circle of hell. The animal torture chamber. The prison from which the only release is death. I didn't want to go.

"Wouldn't it look weird if you bring me there in the middle of the night?"

"Usually no one's there at night. And anyone who was there would understand why a professor would bring a student to see it."

Anyone would understand. How could I say that I didn't?

———

Of course he had a motorcycle. Was there ever a more ridiculous cliché than the hot professor with long hair and aviator glasses, cowboy boots, and a powerful bike? At least, from what I understand, the macho-academic-abuser look has gone out of style.

When I try to remember who I was then, I remember that night when I held on to his waist for dear life. As we flew through the cold night, the streets that I walked along every day could have been streets in a dream, streets in outer space. We rocketed through the darkness. I have never again felt that special, that young, that free.

He parked the bike in his dedicated space outside the psychology building. A dedicated parking space!

A freezing wind was blowing. Icy needles pierced us. I leaned against him. We were lucky it was so cold that no one was likely to be out for a walk. I burrowed under his jacket. It would have looked really bad, I knew. I was hiding. The deeper I pressed my face into his chest, the more invisible I felt.

He said he came here often, several times a week. He'd never brought someone, but he wanted me to see it.

All I heard was: *you are the first*.

————

Not everyone in those days had the heart, the conscience, the consciousness, the fear of disapproval that people have today. The research at our college wasn't just a matter of one-way mirrors and grad students spying on undergrads.

There were laboratories. Animal laboratories.

My first-year roommate dropped out at the end of the first semester because her work-study job had been to clean out the monkey cages. She didn't mind the cleaning part, but she couldn't bear what they did to the monkeys, hooking them up to electrodes and monitoring them around the clock.

It was well known that Professor Muller was researching the effects of sleep deprivation, and the monkeys got a little jolt whenever they dozed off. The lab was Muller's kingdom. He decided what went on there. It was an open secret, but no one mentioned it. Ever.

The labs were in the basement of the psychology building. Sometimes, when the furnaces fired up in the early winter, a ghastly smell seeped up through the classroom floors. Sometimes we could hear dogs bark. Today there would be protests, demonstrations. Concerned students would shut the place down. But not then. We pretended not to smell, not to hear. We went on with our studies.

———

Watching and waiting for the Woman of the Year to taste her delicious walnut-oil-infused salad, I thought, *I'm doing this all wrong. I should have brought a cage of white lab mice and released them at the restaurant.* But what would be the chances that the Woman of the Year would know that I was referencing our college experience? The guests might understand that I was sending a message, but they wouldn't understand the message I was sending.

They'd arrest me as either a crazy person or a passionate animal-rights advocate, or both. What would have been the point? Surely the Woman of the Year was against cruelty to animals and didn't own shares in a beauty product company that allowed animal testing. And how exactly would I smuggle a cage of mice past the hefty bouncers guarding the door and the giraffe girls with their tablets?

I'd wait for the walnut oil to work.

The other guests were thinking happy thoughts, dreaming about their hopes and plans and ambitions, maybe suffering a little social anxiety, probably not all that much.

And me? I was reliving the nightmare of the animal lab at college.

The waking dream of being taken there on a motorcycle by my inappropriate faculty boyfriend.

Chapter Thirteen

I WONDERED WHY Dell was taking me to the animal labs, what he wanted me to see. Or if he just wanted to watch me seeing it. To observe me.

For the first (but not the last) time it crossed my mind that I was one of his experimental subjects. A sidebar or maybe a footnote to the research he was doing on our class.

Standing outside the psych building, I said, "One thing." I still couldn't bring myself to call him by his nickname, so I didn't call him anything. "I'm not going to be able to stand it if there are cats in the lab. I just can't . . ." My head was pressed against his chest for warmth. I had to repeat it several times so he could hear me. Each time I sounded weaker.

"Of course," he said. "Understood. There aren't any cats. A couple of monkeys and some mice. I like to visit the monkeys. Abba and Babba."

"Who named them?" *You named* me, I thought.

"Not me," he said. "Me and the monkeys don't have that kind of relationship. We're just friends."

"Okay," I said. "That's . . . unusual."

———

The smell was overpowering. Every animal that had ever been through that laboratory had left behind the stench of its pain and terror and death. It was stronger than the smell of the lion house at the zoo, or the pet shop, the barn, the stable, the dead skunk on the road. This was worse than roadkill, worse than putrefaction.

I heard water dripping. Scurrying. High-pitched squealing. The scratch scratch scratch of panicked rodents racing desperately around their cages.

It was a horror movie. Except that it was real. I had been brought to this terrible place by a man who—say it!—I was in love with.

If it had been a TV procedural, I would have vomited. And maybe someone watching—me—would have said, "Vomit!" I walked away from Dell and pretended to be coughing and clearing my throat.

It was a test, but what kind? How would I know if I passed or failed?

Dell had brought a red bandanna soaked in lavender water. He tied it around my mouth. He kissed the back of my neck. Right there in the stinky animal lab.

It was the hottest thing ever. The smell of flowers overpowered the smell of fear and death. Or maybe I just thought so.

Dell had brought the lavender-water kerchief to protect me. No one had ever been kinder. No one had ever been so thoughtful. My parents were never that nice. They weren't monsters, but they were cold and unkind. Let's just leave it at that.

I wanted to turn and run out, back into the cold, fresh air. But I needed to show Dell that I was strong enough—tough and grown-up and *professional* enough—to look at whatever he wanted me to see.

The light in the lab was a million times sicklier than the light of the scariest parking garage. A fluorescent bulb sputtered and buzzed, snapping its harsh glare on and off. Water dripped into the metal sink basins, and pipes leaked onto the cement floor. I heard scurrying from across the room. The mice were scratching the floors of their cages.

"Abba and Babba are asleep," Dell said.

He whistled the first bars of the "Ode to Joy" from Beethoven's Ninth Symphony. It must have been their signal. The two monkeys woke up. Their eyelids blinked open. They were overjoyed to see Dell. They babbled—*saying* something, but what?—and jumped up and down as he let them out of their cages.

How had he gotten the keys? It wasn't the moment to ask. He sat in a nearby chair, and the monkeys jumped into his lap. It seemed like a nightmare, but never, not for one second, did I doubt that it was real.

I backed up until I was as far away from the cages as I could get and still be in the room. I didn't care if Dell thought I was weak. I was scared. I couldn't help it. I'd read about monkeys attacking humans, and if any monkeys had a reason to fight back, to make a rush for freedom, these monkeys did.

But as everyone who loves animals knows, they sense when you are their friend. When you want to help them. I'd read about a gray whale that remained perfectly still while a crew of divers freed it from some nets and ropes in which it had gotten trapped. When they freed it, the whale did a happy dance and then swam back and kissed each one of the divers in turn. I saw a TV show about a guy freeing a wild hawk whose wing got snagged on barbed wire, and the hawk just sat there and let the guy work. When I found Pyewacket in the street drug market, he never once shied or struggled or tried to scratch me. He understood right away. He gave himself over to me the moment I lifted him up and away from the syringe on the ground. He curled up into my hands like a furry ball of pure love.

Standing there in the animal lab, I tried not to think about my cat.

The monkeys bumped shoulders with Dell, like old drinking buddies bellying up to a bar.

"This is Abba. And this is Babba. And this is Lorelei."

In that hellish situation, amid those repulsive surroundings, I still nearly fainted with pleasure just because he'd said my name. I nodded hello to the monkeys, who had been in those cramped cages in this horrible prison. I longed to set them free forever. I should have grabbed them and run as fast as I could.

But I didn't intervene. I didn't move. I was there as Dell's guest. Dell said, "Watch this."

He flipped a switch, and a screen lit up. He reached into a drawer beneath a table and took out a video game console with two remotes. He gave one to the bigger monkey. Abba. The male.

"Game on," he said, and the words *NBA Basketball* flashed onto the screen.

"Abba always plays the Celts," said Dell. "This time I'm the Lakers."

I watched, in shock, as the monkey played against my teacher.

Human fingers, primate fingers, trembled and dove and punched the keys. A crowd roared on the audio track while the strident electronic announcers kept score.

Dell played well. I wanted him to play well. To win. I don't know why it mattered, but it did. It was crazy, I knew, but I didn't want a guy I was sleeping with to be crappy at video games. In hindsight, that makes me think that I deserved everything I got.

Dell was good. He held his own. But the monkey was better. Faster. Smarter.

I have never fully recovered from the surreal strangeness of watching a man with whom I was in love play and lose a video game with a pair of monkeys.

The monkey bared his teeth and jumped up and down when he won by fourteen points.

"You beat me fair and square," Dell said. "Again." He grabbed the monkey's shoulder and squeezed it.

"Good work," he said. Then to me, "He always wins."

I said, "I can't believe it." I couldn't. What demented genius had taught the monkeys to play—and win at—video games?

"Believe what you see," Dell said. "That's the first rule of science. Horse, not zebra."

And what did I see? Dell and the monkeys were friends. Maybe he was their only human friend. He was important to them. He was on their side. They looked forward to his visits. Short of setting them free, he was doing the next best thing.

He'd filled his pockets with fruit and cookies for the monkeys.

"Diabetic cookies," he told me. "No sugar. Abba and Babba prefer them."

The monkeys shrieked with pleasure as they ate the fruit and cookies.

He kissed each monkey on its forehead. They let themselves be kissed, then went willingly into their cages. He shut the door and locked up.

"See you tomorrow," he said.

"Why don't we set them free?" I said.

"We can't," he said. "Not yet. In the future. But believe me, I think about it. I think about it all the time."

I wanted him thinking about *me* all the time. I knew that could never happen. I loved him more for it—for all of it. He wasn't just the coolest teacher and the best lover, but he cared deeply about these poor suffering creatures.

I said nothing, I did nothing. I told no one, though I would have loved to tell Holly. But I didn't. I didn't.

I tried not to wonder where this was leading.

I went to class. I said nothing. I played my secret games with Dell.

———

Not that long ago, a group of Woodward students staged a hunger strike in the animal lab. By the time the protesting students had gotten visibly skinnier, and their parents were threatening to with-hold tuition, the lab was shut down forever.

I remember, also around that same time, seeing a death notice for Professor Muller.

DR. OTTO MULLER, EXPERT ON PRIMATE BEHAVIOR, 88.

Professor Muller died of heart failure at his home in Great Bar-rington, Massachusetts. He had been ailing for some time after a freak accident while on safari in Africa. His wife and daughter having predeceased him, he is survived by his only son, Otto.

The newspaper must have gotten that wrong. I distinctly remembered that the boy—the boy who fainted at the Thanksgiving dinner table—had been renamed and was going by the name of Paul.

I wondered what the professor's accident was. I liked to think it was a lioness taking revenge for whatever happened in that lab.

Chapter Fourteen

A DISTURBANCE RIPPLED the air of the Woman of the Year gala dinner. You could feel it on your skin, like just before a thunderstorm. They say you can feel the hair on your arms stand up, but that evening I couldn't feel the hairs on my arms—tightly swaddled by the sleeves of my uncomfortable black dress—at all. Did my right sleeve smell of walnut oil? I couldn't exactly sniff my arm. I really should have left the dinner by then, but I couldn't move.

My Barbie wig was beginning to itch. I'd begun to think that if something didn't happen soon, if she didn't eat her salad, or if the walnut oil didn't bother her, or if she'd been lying all this time about her allergy to nuts, I would leave and wait for another chance to semi-poison the Woman of the Year.

That was when I felt that electrical charge go through the room. It's how our limbic brains warn us: *Don't turn that corner, there's a street fight on that block. Don't step in front of that car.* I guess I remember something from my brief career as a psychology major.

———

Actually, I remember a lot. Not that it helps me. I tried to draw on my knowledge of psychology to ease the pain of the people I had to fire at my job, but I hadn't learned enough, and anyway, it was useless. Maybe I would have made a crappy therapist. I never got to find out.

Firing all those people, because I was told to, because I had to, to keep my job, that was the worst thing I'd done.

Until now.

Now I was doing something really wrong . . . or maybe not all that wrong. Maybe half the people in this room thought Holly had it coming. Who talks about herself for twenty minutes? Were the other guests really that starstruck?

A buzz rose from the crowd. Something was happening up front, centered around . . . the head table. Oh no! *Could it be the Woman of the Year?*

Well, yes, it could be. If things have gone right, it could be.

No one knew what the problem was. No one knew but me. If I'd gotten lucky. Unless there was some huge coincidence and another guest was having "difficulties," things were looking up.

Did people push forward to see what was going on? No, they did not. This was a civilized crowd. They stayed back, waiting, like grown-ups, though a young woman in a tiny red dress and extremely high heels tottered past me, murmuring, "I'm a doctor. I'm an MD."

Then the rumor began to spread, first in whispers, then louder.

Holly Serpenta had suffered some sort of attack. The Woman of the Year had fallen! The standing crowd made it impossible to see. Why couldn't they sit down?

Anaphylactic. The word bounced around the room. *Anaphy-lactic shock.* Everyone knew what that meant. Probably most of them knew about Holly's nut allergy. Perhaps some of them were here because of Holly's nut allergy foundation.

Then I heard someone say, "It's cool. Her PA has an EpiPen."

The crowd held its collective breath, followed by a collective sigh of relief.

This was all my doing! It was hard not to feel proud of having upstaged the Woman of the Year. I reminded myself that I'd probably done something illegal, which just shows how little our legal system has to do with justice.

No one knew whether to stick around or leave. No one left, though they should have. Give Holly some breathing room! But the crowd felt they had to stay there—for Holly! Shoulder to shoulder, the well-wishers wanted to help, and the nakedly curious—the rubberneckers at car wrecks—wanted to see what would happen.

God knows what those people had done to make their money, bankers and real estate speculators, CEOs of companies that donated to the Woman of the Year Foundation and destroyed entire small countries.

But I was probably the only one who had poisoned an actual person, close-up and personal, in the actual room.

I had the mark of Cain on my forehead now, half obscured by the longish bangs of my Barbie wig.

Someone said the EMT squad had been called, and we waited outside the room. We'd cheer them on. Like sports fans. We'd supervise. Like useless family members. The squad would be glad to see us. Then everyone just sat back down, stuck around, for Holly, who totally didn't need us. Were her eyes open? I couldn't see. No one asked.

When they finally arrived, the EMT workers—two women and two men, all dressed like firefighters—saw us as a wall of flesh to get through, a Red Sea of gawkers to be parted. Where did they learned to do their super macho, conquering-hero entrance? Like male strippers swarming a bachelorette party, not that I'd ever been to one.

Pushing heavy equipment—a collapsible gurney—they stormed in past the lectern. No giraffe girls looked up *their* names on an electronic tablet.

They disappeared into the restaurant. We could see their helmets rise and dip each time they grabbed some new tool or machine. Ages later, they wheeled Holly out, strapped to the gurney, tilted back, diagonal to the floor. She looked like a medieval torture victim about to be broken on a wheel. A prisoner about to be waterboarded, a kidnapped girl about to be eaten by Hannibal Lecter.

In fact, she looked like Hannibal Lecter.

For the first time, I felt guilty. Sorry for what I'd done.

A little guilty. A little sorry.

Let the punishment fit the crime.

What she'd done to me was worse.

Much worse.

Holly would be fine.

Her eyes were open. She looked around. I wanted to wave as she passed. Cheerio! I controlled myself. A few people did wave, weakly. Did they think this was a parade?

I wondered if she'd vomited. I would never know.

Chapter Fifteen

I HATE HOW holidays mark time. They tell you when things happened.

I should have known that the Thanksgiving of my senior year would be go badly.

The problem was that I was having a secret affair with my teacher. On the phone, as Mom and I made our sad little plans for the holiday, I could tell that my mother, who never paid any attention, could tell that something was going on. Dad never noticed anything, which made Mom hate him more.

I traveled home by Greyhound bus with Pyewacket in a carrier. The driver, steaming in his personal cloud of menthol cough drops, made me show my doctor's letter saying that I needed a comfort animal.

That seemed like a bad sign. I wish I could have taken Pyewacket out of his cage and snuggled him against my chest to calm the suspicion that my mother was lying in wait for me, preparing to attack.

I should have known that her ill will would collect around Pyewacket. My weak spot. She knew that he occupied the part of my heart that was still open and undefended. The part that she and my dad had never cared enough to claim.

My parents said they couldn't pick me up at the bus station, so I took a cab. Mom was waiting for me in the doorway. She seemed to have grown older and harsher looking in the few months since I'd seen her last, and the house looked smaller and more decrepit.

"You know your dad's been sick" was the first thing she said.

"No," I said. "I didn't."

I'd talked to my parents the day before on the phone. Why didn't anyone tell me? Was it so bad that they were waiting to break the news in person? Even with all our problems, and despite my mixed feelings about my dad, I was terrified. I didn't want to lose him.

"Respiratory stuff," said Mom.

"Respiratory stuff? What does that mean?"

"Pulmonary. If he keeps it up, he'll be carrying around an oxygen tank, and I'll be the one who has to make sure it's filled and the hoses work."

I was weak-kneed with relief. Nothing all that terrible was happening—at least not right now. "Well, sure. He smokes two packs a day."

"Nothing to do about that, at this late date. Asthma, COPD, he's got it, the whole nine yards. Anyway, his doctor says he needs to keep away from pet dander." She looked meaningfully at Pyewacket's carrier. "Your cat can't be in the house. Not inside. I'm sorry."

I'd just gotten there. I hadn't even let him out of his cage. We hadn't even said hello.

"What am I supposed to do with him this weekend?" I was sure I could talk her out of it, but I was tired from the bus trip.

Mom said, "I thought that maybe she could stay in the garage."

"He," I said. "Pyewacket is a he."

"Right. I knew that."

"It's freezing in there. He'd be miserable. He could die of cold."

"I think we have a space heater somewhere . . ." Mom looked around, as if a heater might materialize at any moment.

Maybe that was what did it. What set me off. I'm not an impulsive person. I never wanted to hurt my parents, even after all the ways they'd hurt me. Pyewacket's life was something else.

I said, "Is Dad really that ill, or are you just messing with me because you can?"

Mom looked shocked, not because I would suggest such as thing, but because—I was sure—I'd found her out.

Something came over me. One of those moments people describe and you never quite believe. People say, *Something came over me. Suddenly, I had superhuman strength and I lifted the car off the baby.* Or: *Something came over me. I'd never shoplifted before.*

I picked up Pyewacket's carrier, grabbed my little wheelie, called for a cab, and went back to the bus station and bought a ticket to my college.

Mom didn't try to stop me. She never even asked if I wanted to come inside and get warm and have a drink or snack and use the bathroom. She didn't ask if I wanted to say hello and goodbye to Dad.

I was in a weirdly good mood, all the way back to school. I felt exhilarated. Set free.

None of it was my fault. My mother hadn't wanted me there. She knew I wouldn't stay if they didn't let me keep my cat inside. I imagined waking up and finding Pyewacket frozen stiff in the garage.

No one I knew would be at school. Holly was meeting her parents at an aunt's in Chicago. It was completely fine with me to spend the holiday alone with Pyewacket, the two of us in our apartment. It would be less lonely than being at my parents' house, especially if I had to be without him, fearing for his comfort—his life.

Well, I knew one person at school. Dell was staying around. He had some writing to do. It says something, that I didn't feel comfortable letting him know that I was back in town. I was trying so hard not to seem like your typical college student having trouble with her parents.

I was glad I lived in an apartment. It was so much better than an empty dorm.

Okay. I'll admit I did think, *Maybe I'll run into Dell*.

He'd never given me his phone number. I'd never asked. Was it strange, having sex with a person I didn't know how to reach? That, too, was a turn on, though now it seems hard to believe. I didn't know what was strange or not. I'd done whatever I thought Dell wanted.

I let Pyewacket out of the carrier as soon as we got back to our apartment. He was overjoyed to be home. He ran to all his favorite places, scratched the leg of his favorite chair, drank a bowl of water, slurped up a smaller bowl of milk, peed in his box, ate a whole can of food, and trotted over to cuddle goodbye when I went out to get some groceries.

It was out of my way to pass the psychology building on my way to the grocery. In fact, it wasn't on the way at all. But that was how I went.

The campus was dark and empty. I wasn't scared. Maybe I would see him. I would figure out what to say, depending on whether or not he looked happy to see me.

Oh, I was just taking a walk. Oh, I decided not to go home for the holiday. Oh, I was so surprised to see him! As if I hadn't been willing him to be there, wanting to run into him.

I would admit that I'd had an argument with my mother. Maybe he would feel sorry for me. Maybe he'd want to console me and come over to my apartment. Why did I always feel like he was doing me a favor?

His motorcycle was parked outside. I grabbed a lamppost to steady myself.

His office window was lit.

If sleeping with a guy didn't give me the right to knock on his door, I shouldn't have been sleeping with him. I didn't want that to be true, so I knocked.

He opened the door, alert and on edge. Who was there, at this hour? Only now did I realize how late it was. I hadn't noticed. I'd been back and forth to my parents' house and had stopped off at home to feed Pyewacket.

"Lorelei!" Was he glad or just surprised? "What are you doing here?"

I told him my whole sad story. Staying home might have meant Pyewacket freezing to death. My mother wanted my cat to freeze. She'd always been like that.

By that point I was crying. He put his arms around me.

He rode me home on his motorcycle.

He parked his bike and came upstairs. What did my landlady think, my professor and I riding up on his motorcycle the night before Thanksgiving?

He could never have touched me that way if he hadn't loved me. Afterward we lay in bed and laughed and each drank a shot of bourbon.

He'd almost finished getting dressed when he looked back at me, naked under the sheet, and said, "I don't suppose you've got plans for Thanksgiving dinner?"

Was he asking me to spend the holiday with him? That seemed too impossibly good to be true.

"No," I said. "But that's okay. I'll buy a can of turkey for Pyewacket, and we'll celebrate together."

I knew I sounded pathetic. Probably I meant to.

He said, "I'm going to Professor Muller's house for dinner. Why don't you come with me?"

The idea was terrifying. I desperately longed to say no.

"Yes," I said. "I'd love to."

Chapter Sixteen

PROFESSOR MULLER'S house sat like a giant brick battleship docked on a large suburban lawn.

If I'd been scared about the evening ahead, the house ramped up my terror. But I couldn't chicken out. I wanted Dell to think I was brave. He couldn't imagine the courage it took for me to act as if going to Professor Muller's house for Thanksgiving was the most natural thing in the world. Maybe he knew how uneasy I was—and he was testing me. I would fail if I went and made a fool of myself. I would fail if I was too scared to go. It was a lose-lose situation.

It was too late to back out now. If I was going to say no, I should have done it when Dell asked me and not now, standing at the end of the walkway that led to Professor's Muller's door.

The house was dark and looked deserted. Did we have the wrong night? How could we? It was Thanksgiving.

"Are they home?" I'd murmured as I got off Dell's bike and gave him my helmet to stow. "Are you sure they're expecting us?"

"The dining room's in back," he said. "They keep the rooms dark unless they're actually using them. Muller's a maniac about not wasting electricity. It's just another way the guy is years ahead of his time." I'd noticed it before: the reverence and awe that crept into Dell's voice when he talked about Professor Muller. There was no one else he spoke of like that. It never failed to surprise me.

I was even more surprised that Dell had a key to the professor's front door. I had lots of questions I couldn't ask. I wasn't sure I wanted answers. I imagined Dell and Professor Muller working together on animal experiments. I imagined, in the basement of this huge house, a secret lab, more extreme than the one in the psych building. Maybe Dell had taken me there to prepare me for this one.

I told myself: *Relax. You're going to a Thanksgiving dinner, not a torture chamber.*

Dell said, "The family has a house on the Cape. They often go away on weekends. They gave me the key so I could look in on the place when they're gone. It's the least I could do, considering how much the professor has done for me."

What exactly Professor Muller had done for Dell was another question I couldn't ask.

I tripped as we walked up the dark front steps, and Dell took my hand to steady me. I felt bereft when he let go.

On both sides of the front door were stone lions with weeds sprouting from their backs. Planters. I wondered what Mrs. Muller was like, and if the house would have seemed less threatening on a bright spring morning.

Dell had told me that Professor Muller had two children, a girl and a boy, and that on holidays they welcomed faculty members who were stranded at school or who lived alone.

Like Dell.

"Will there be other people besides us and the family?" I longed for a crowd in which to disappear. But Dell's bike was the only vehicle parked outside. A stucco garage stood alongside the house, its door shut.

"Do they know that you're bringing me?"

"Yes, of course. It's fine. Professor Muller likes to keep in touch with the undergraduate population."

The undergraduate population? Was that what I meant to Dell? I needed to stop thinking that way. It was making me more insecure.

Dell took my hand again and led me through the dark house. I smelled more than I saw. Carpet dust. Furniture polish. An edge of mildew. The Mullers had school-age children. But it smelled like the house of two old people living alone. No pets, no kids' books, no toys.

We walked toward the light, toward a doorway. Only the dining room was lit by a weak chandelier. The heavy dark furniture, the enormous sideboard covered by a lace runner, the glass-fronted cabinet filled with shepherd and shepherdess figurines, seemed to have been imported from the home of a wealthy, traditional family in prewar . . . Vienna.

Of course. Professor Muller was Viennese.

The family was already at the table. Were we late?

I could tell that Dell didn't think so. The professor, his wife, and their two children didn't seem surprised to see us. No one smiled. No one got up. They murmured their hellos so quietly I could hardly hear them. Then they went back to staring down at their plates.

The Addams family, I thought.

They could have been mannequins in a store window. It was like a set for a play. Or for a horror movie: Thanksgiving dinner of the dead.

Professor Muller sat at the head of the table. Seated on his right, his wife—his second, younger wife, I'd heard—had tightly curled blond hair and the saucy look of a film star or a pinup. Bright red lipstick enlarged her thin mouth, and she wore a coral-pink cashmere sweater, pearls, the style of fifty years ago.

As little as I knew about adults, I thought she seemed a little high-strung.

Across from her sat the children, a little girl of about fourteen who looked and dressed like a teenaged replica of her mother, and a boy of nine or ten.

The boy was gawky, twitchy, with skin so pale it looked blue, highlighting the glistening scatters of acne across both cheeks. He was at that awkward stage when boys get plump in preparation for growing taller. He wore thick glasses, and his face was unusually long, as if his features had been stretched like taffy. He tilted his head at a listening angle even when everyone was silent. He wore a jacket and tie, and his neck stuck out of his collar in a way that made me think of toothpaste squeezed from a tube.

The kids stole a glance at me and Dell, then went back to staring at their plates, ashamed, as if they'd been caught looking at something forbidden.

The silent tableau creaked into action. Professor Muller smiled at Dell, a smile so strained it seemed it might actually hurt.

The professor was wearing his eye patch.

"Welcome," he said. "To our happy home."

He drew out the word *haaappppy*, so we knew he was joking.

"This is Lorelei Green," said Dell.

"Lorelei," said the professor. "A beautiful German name."

For a moment I was afraid that Dell was going to say that he'd named me. But of course he didn't. That might have revealed too much. Still . . . what did the professor and his family think that Dell was doing at their house with a student on the back of his motorcycle—on Thanksgiving evening? I didn't want them to know the truth. It would have been embarrassing. Dell might have gotten into trouble, though I doubted that. Things were different then, and clearly he had the department chairman on his side.

"Say Happy Thanksgiving to Miss Green," said the professor. "Millie?"

"Happy Thanksgiving, Miss Green," said the girl.

"Paul?"

"Happy Thanksgiving, Miss Green," said the boy.

"Happy Thanksgiving, Millie and Paul," I said.

The professor glared at me. Was I not supposed to say their names?

"And you already know Professor Randall, children."

"Happy Thanksgiving, Professor Randall," the children said in unison.

"Nice to see you again," mumbled Millie.

"What?" said her father. "We can't hear you."

"It's nice to see you again," said Millie, a little louder.

"It's nice to see you, too, Millie and Paul," said Dell warmly. "Happy Thanksgiving to you both."

The children glanced at me and looked down again. Their mother did the same.

"No one should be alone on a day like this," Professor Muller said. In theory that explained what I was doing there, enough so that everyone could relax. But the mood remained tense.

How I missed Pyewacket! I wanted to hold him against me. I wanted to feel his steady reassurance whirring near my heart.

"I was just telling Paul and Millie the latest news from Abba and Babba," said Professor Muller. "I have been encouraging our primate friends to watch TV so I can find out what they like best. And do you know what they prefer?"

Everyone shook their heads no. Even Dell and I, though he wasn't asking us.

After a silence, the girl said, "What?"

"Complete sentences, please." Her mother's voice cut through the hush.

"What did the primates prefer?" Millie said.

"What what?" said her father.

The girl clenched her eyes shut. "What TV program did the primates prefer?"

"They preferred the live feed from my office. The video of me eating lunch."

His bark-like laugh rattled deep in his chest, ghostly and alarming. "Further evidence, in case you children need it, that television will reduce your intelligence to that of a primate."

"Higher primates," said the boy.

Silence.

"What did you say?" asked his father.

"Aren't chimps among the higher primates?"

"We've talked about that," said his father.

Then the boy did a strange thing. His head drifted down onto his empty plate. We all stared at him for a moment, until he picked his head up again and gazed off into the distance.

Dell and I were still standing.

"We seem to have quite forgotten our hostly duties. Isn't that right, my dear?"

Mrs. Muller nodded miserably.

"Sit down," the professor said to us. "Please."

The only empty chairs were at the opposite end of the table. I was glad to be far from the professor. The room was stuffy and overheated. I sank into my chair, grateful and slightly unsteady.

"Would you do the honors, dear?" Professor Muller asked his wife.

Mrs. Muller stood: a skeleton in an expensive cashmere sweater. I held my breath as she picked up the carving knife. Suddenly I felt certain that she wanted to plunge it into her husband's heart. Where had *that* thought come from? The mood was formal, even a little . . . spooky, but no darker than my own childhood Thanksgivings: Dad drinking too much, getting stupid, my parents fighting.

Professor Muller cleared his throat.

"Well then, Paul, tell us, what are we *celebrating*?" He stressed the last word, again in case anyone didn't know he was joking.

The boy said nothing.

Mrs. Muller dropped her knife, which clattered against the platter. She rushed off toward what I assumed was the kitchen. A flickering light went on, followed by the crashing and banging of someone searching for something.

Mrs. Muller reappeared with an electric knife.

She poised it over the turkey. Its buzz was as loud as a chain saw.

"Dear, that simply has to stop," Professor Muller told his wife. Not gently, not harshly. Instructionally. Like a strict parent.

She turned off the electric knife and picked up the carving knife again.

"Paul?" prompted his father.

"The Pilgrims," said Paul.

Mrs. Muller stopped carving.

"Complete sentences, please." She sounded threatening.

Professor Muller said, "As I'm sure you remember, Professor Randall, we ask that the children speak in complete sentences. If they don't, they don't eat. It works remarkably well to turn them into civilized human beings. Or at least to make them *behave* like civilized human beings."

"I remember," said Dell. His voice was toneless. I glanced at him. Was starving the children unless they spoke in complete sentences really okay with him? His face told me less than nothing.

"We are celebrating the pilgrims' arrival in the New World," muttered the boy.

Professor Muller leaned back in his chair.

"Ah yes," he said. "We are honoring the white imperialist pilgrims who stole the land of the Indigenous people."

His wife frowned as she sawed at the turkey. Maybe the knife wasn't sharp enough. At least my parents had that together. My father carved, and even with his shaky hands, it usually went pretty well.

"The Puritans were our earliest successful experiment in American mind control," said Professor Muller. "Scare an entire population senseless, make them see hell more closely and vividly than their own front parlor, and they will do anything— *anything*—you want. They will burn their mother at the stake if she challenges the mindless obedience of the community."

Dell seemed to have forgotten me. He was listening to Professor Muller. I couldn't tell what he was thinking.

"The turkey is hideously undercooked." Mrs. Muller had arranged the turkey on a platter, and now she was poking at it, in obvious distaste, with the tip of her carving knife. "Just as we all knew it would be. As it is, every year. I wanted to leave the bird in the oven longer, but my husband has very definite, very *adamant* opinions about when it should be taken out. Sometimes I have the feeling that he *wants* to undercook it on purpose so he can perform a little science experiment, watching his family and friends eat undercooked turkey without complaining."

Wow. A long silence followed that. The easiest thing was to look down at my plate, like the others.

I believed the professor's wife. The meat was nearly raw. She knew better. The knife was kept purposely dull. She knew better than that too. We were his experiments. He watched how we handled stress.

I was doing okay, considering. Holidays were always strange, but this was one of the strangest.

Dell had brought me. He wanted me here. That gave me the courage to face it.

Like the evil husband in a black-and-white film, Professor Muller said, "My wife has quite an imagination." How many times had I heard that line? Were we supposed to laugh? Dell made that funny snort. Mrs. Muller glared at him, then turned and glared at her husband.

Plates of food were passed around. One stopped in front of me. I wondered how, if not on purpose, you could ruin every component of a Thanksgiving dinner. The mashed potatoes were cold and watery, the gravy oily and lumpy, the vegetables cooked gray. Even the jellied canned cranberry sauce had a fizzy vinegar edge.

No one spoke as we ate. I managed to get some of the awful

food down. Though we sat side by side, I sensed a chasm opening up and widening between me and Dell.

———

I remember the dinner lasting forever, but two events have stuck with me, surfacing from that dismal swamp of a holiday meal.

The first involved the boy. Suddenly, out of nowhere, he said something about the food, something along the lines of "These peas are mushy."

Gluey was more like it. But this wasn't a house where you said that.

His parents and sister put down their forks. Dell and I did the same.

The only sound was the ticking clock. Professor Muller stared at his son. He focused on him for a very long time. Even from the far end of the table I felt the heat of that one eye, felt the beam of its harsh brightness searching out the child.

His blazing, one-eyed gaze didn't waver until at last the boy screamed—a sharp hoarse animal cry wrenched from deep inside his chest.

The boy slipped sideways and fell off his chair. He slowly slid and crumpled down onto the carpet.

I started to stand. My instinct was to do something. I wanted to help somehow. But Dell gently took my shoulder and eased me back in my seat.

"Not to worry," said the boy's father.

The boy's family let him lie on the floor. Minutes went by.

I felt the strangest sensation, a wracking and violent bodily chill, as if someone had opened all the doors and windows at once. A cold wind blew across my shoulders and up my back. I wrapped my arms around myself and shivered. I had the sensation that someone was running a dripping ice cube up and down my spine. At least I was still wearing my jacket, which no one had offered to take. I wound my scarf around my neck, but it didn't help. Why didn't anyone else seem cold? Was I the only one?

Ticktock said the cuckoo clock on the wall.

I couldn't tell how much time was passing. *Ticktock. Ticktock.* Forever.

"It happens," said Mrs. Muller, not directly to me or Dell, vaguely in our direction. "Paul is a very high-strung little boy. Anything can set him off."

It wasn't *anything*. It was his father. His father's terrifying face. But it wasn't my place to say that. I was the guest; Dell had brought me along. The boy's father hadn't touched him. It wasn't as if we'd witnessed a beating.

If the professor's great subject, his expertise, was mind control, it had already worked on me. I let a child lie on the floor, and I did and said nothing.

It *was* the Milgram pain experiment. Maybe we hadn't given the boy an electric shock, but I hadn't stopped this.

Obedience to authority. I'd failed. I'd given Professor Muller some useful data.

We sat there. Eating or pretending to eat, while a child lay on the floor unconscious.

Everything that happened to me was punishment for that. But how could I have stopped it?

I attacked the turkey, cutting around the raw parts, hiding the gristly carnage under the burned Brussels sprouts and watery mashed potatoes.

Dr. Muller cut his meat and vegetables, forked up his potatoes. He ate everything on his plate, smacking his lips with gusto.

The boy still lay on the floor. Shouldn't someone call a doctor?

I still felt cold. Freezing. Dell didn't seem to notice that I had been shivering all this time.

Just when I was starting to think that it might be up to me to save him, the boy moaned softly. Moments later he sat up, hoisted himself onto his chair, and resumed sluggishly eating his dinner as if nothing unusual had happened.

"I trust that you're all right?" said his father.

"Rested, actually," said the boy.

"What?" said his mother.

"I'm actually rested," said the boy.

As Professor Muller sighed deeply and settled back into his chair, I felt as if my chilled body might be returning to something near normal temperature.

Professor Muller went on as if nothing had happened. "Almost every day, I think about what it means to believe, as few people do, in a combination of behaviorism and eugenics. Of course the latter field has fallen into total disrepute after those madmen in Germany ruined things for everyone. Eugenics! You can't even *say* the word, you certainly can't teach a course in it except to denounce it as evil. But in my opinion the jury is still out.

"I have always believed in the combination of eugenics and behaviorism as our best shot, perhaps our only shot, at perfecting the race. Behaviorism is the more compassionate, gentler approach to eugenics. First you try behavior modification. You give the maladjusted a chance to function like normal individuals. You condition them to respond in the most mature and useful ways. You train them to act like people. Shock them lightly when they don't get it, but only in extreme cases. And if that doesn't work, well . . ."

The professor smiled a tad more broadly this time and shrugged. A little *mocking* shrug. What can you do?

"Needless to say, I am joking. As you know."

I hadn't known that he was joking. Was he joking now?

"The problem is that you can't predict the outcomes in real-world situations. I married my wife because I imagined that we would have two children who looked like her.

"And I did get one." He nodded at his pretty daughter. "What I didn't know, what I couldn't have predicted, was that there had been some very weak and stupid people in my wife's family line, traits that only revealed themselves . . ."

He nodded at his son.

No one spoke. No one moved. He had just called his wife and son stupid in front of us. But we were in his house, at his table.

This was one of those moments when I experienced what it meant—what it really meant—to be an empath. I felt the boy's humiliation, his loneliness, his pain. I felt his emotions as if they were my own. I felt almost drunk with it, that swimmy out-of-body sensation that sometimes signals that I've had too much wine. Suddenly queasy, I picked up my glass and gulped down the brackish warm water until the moment passed. I grabbed the table and steadied myself.

No one—not even Dell—seemed to notice.

Professor Muller was still talking about his son. "His real name is Otto. Otto Junior. That's how much I was counting on a near duplicate of myself. Or anyway, a recognizable version of my better qualities."

He laughed his mirthless chuckle. "But it was rapidly obvious that the name wasn't . . . right. We would have to rename him."

Was Dell thinking what I was thinking? He had renamed *me*. Was that something he'd learned from his mentor? For the first time I wondered, *What kind of person thinks they have the right to change someone's name?* The Mullers had named their son in the first place and later changed their minds. But by then he knew his name as Otto. What had it meant to go from being Otto to being Paul? Was he relieved not to have to bear the burden of his father's name? He'd fainted under his father's stare. What else had his family done to him?

"For a while we called him Ojun, short for Otto Junior. But then my dear wife recalled that Ojun sounded like the name of her family's prize pig back home in Slovakia."

"Slovenia," said Mrs. Muller.

"What?" her husband said.

"I grew up in Slovenia."

"Forgive my failing memory," said her husband. "In any case, you can't go calling your only son after a giant pig. So we called him Juno for a while, but that of course is a girl's name, and if you believe in conditioning, as I do . . . well. I hoped that invoking the name of the goddess of wisdom might offset his feminine qualities, but there was no predicting.

"So we settled on Paul. We call him Paul, hoping that, like Saul, our son will experience the physically harmless equivalent of falling off his horse on the road to Damascus. Seeing the light and becoming Saint Paul. Which, to be totally frank, I don't see in my son's future. But I don't suppose that one can return one's offspring just because the experiment hasn't worked out."

It was clear that he'd said this before. It was not the first time his family had heard the "joke" about sending his son back to wherever he had come from.

I liked to think that I had some courage. Some Integrity. I'd stood up for bullied kids in grade school, protected the homely sad girls from the mean girls in junior high.

Maybe I would have done something, said something . . . except that I was distracted by something else that had just happened.

———

It had happened when the boy had fainted and was still lying on the ground.

We were eating, or pretending to eat. The room was silent again except for the sounds of cutting and chewing, silverware scraping china.

But those weren't the only sounds.

From time to time the professor and each member of his family made that funny little snort, the sound that Dell made, as his students knew, in class. The sound that, as only I knew, he made in bed.

The sound went around the table, in intervals, orchestrated. Like music. The professor and his wife and two children and Dell made that funny snort.

Professor Muller nodded, and I knew: it was something he had taught them to do.

A sound he'd conditioned them to make.

It is always a shock when something you thought was personal turns out to belong to a group. I was Dell's experiment, and he was Professor Muller's.

———

At last the evening ended and we said our goodbyes. Neither the professor nor his wife rose from the table to see us out. They remained where we'd found them, contemplating the sticky crumbs of a sickeningly sweet, soggy pumpkin pie.

"Thank you," I said, more to the air than to either host.

"It was a pleasure," Professor Muller said coldly.

"Thank you for coming," droned his wife and children, one by one.

Dell drove me home on his motorcycle.

I asked if he wanted to come in. He said he had work to do.

Who works on Thanksgiving night? A scientist, I thought. I hoped.

Somehow I knew what it meant. I don't know how I knew, but I did.

Our affair was over. Ended. He would never come see me again.

The only time we'd be in the same room would be in class.

Having learned to pretend that nothing was going on between us, now I would have to pretend that "nothing" hadn't ended. I would have to pretend that my heart wasn't broken.

Already I longed for him. I missed him. And none of it could be discussed.

"Good night," I said.

"See you in class," he said. "Enjoy the rest of your weekend."

———

Now there's a word for it.

Ghosted.

The person disappears.

Now it's all about devices. The person stops calling or texting. The person doesn't answer your texts. Or the person is weirdly unavailable when you finally get through and try to arrange a date.

Not that I could have phoned Dell. Not that I ever did.

Now they say: *You've been ghosted.* A person has turned into a ghost.

But Dell was still my teacher. He would have to give me a grade at the end of the semester. I couldn't believe that I was worried about that, along with everything else.

I hadn't completely lost my mind. I wanted to graduate.

Even when he stopped coming to my apartment, stopped sleeping with me, stopped bringing me vampire tulips, stopped making me think we had a secret, even then he was still my teacher.

I saw him in class. I got nothing from him. No recognition of what had happened. Not a clue.

Another sign of how young I was was that I didn't think I could ask him. I didn't think I had the right to bring it up. At first I wasn't sure he'd ended it. But when weeks went by without him visiting, I had to admit it was true. It was over. We weren't "taking a break."

I couldn't imagine what I'd done wrong. First he was there, then he wasn't. Was it something I'd said? Was it the dinner at Professor Muller's? Did Dell not want to go on sleeping with someone who had seen him do nothing to help a boy who'd collapsed? Who just sat there beside him in silence as the professor joked about wanting to return his son, the failed eugenics experiment?

Had Professor Muller disapproved of me? Disliked me? Did he tell Dell to break it off? Would Dell have done that if he was asked to?

That would have meant that Dell had never really cared about me—which was seeming more and more likely. I *couldn't* have said anything wrong at that dinner because I didn't say anything at all. Maybe that was the problem. Maybe I'd been too quiet.

In class I focused on staying calm. On acting "normal." On pretending to be the same person I was before: unchanged, untroubled, unbothered. I talked a little more about my cat. Maybe I wanted Dell, the others—and myself—to know there was a creature I loved and who loved me. I remember making up a dream that I hadn't really had, telling the class about being sure that Pyewacket and I had had the same dream.

So many things are embarrassing when you think about them later.

What was I thinking? That Dell would fall back in love with me for having shared a dream with my cat? *Back* in love with me? Had he ever loved me in the first place?

I wished that I could have told Holly. I wished that I'd told her before. I wouldn't blame her for being angry that I'd kept my relationship with Dell a secret. I wouldn't blame her for feeling betrayed. But I still couldn't bring myself to face that it was over, and that I had abandoned her for a man who had now abandoned me.

I wished I had someone to talk to. There was no one I could tell, except Pyewacket, who missed Dell too. Sometimes I caught him waiting by the door, and I knew he was wondering where Dell was. I cried into his fur, and we comforted each other.

Almost every night I had nightmares about pointless confusing journeys. I dreamed I was lost in foreign cities. I needed someone to rescue me, but no one ever came. Some students discussed their dreams in class. But I never talked about those.

One afternoon, as I was coming home from the laundromat, Mrs. O'Neal's door opened and her gray head popped out.

"Laura Lee." That's what she'd heard my parents call me, and that was what she called me, no matter how I often I reminded her that I was Lorelei. "Laura Lee, I hope you don't mind, but that nice girl with the freckles, your friend, that girl—"

My friend? I only had one girl friend. Or at least I used to. Only one who ever came here.

"Holly?" I said.

"Holly. That's it. Very polite young lady! I'd seen her come in with you many times. Not so much lately. But anyway, she said she'd been ringing your bell, and you weren't home.

"She was in tears. She'd left a term paper at your house that she needed to hand in today. She'd fail her course if she didn't get her paper in. I gave her your keys. I hope you don't mind. I told her to leave them outside my door. I made sure she wasn't up there for very long. I was sure it would be okay."

I *did* mind. I minded a lot. Holly hadn't left any term papers at my apartment. Even though she was still, in theory, my friend, I felt . . . invaded.

Maybe she needed to use the bathroom. Of course! No one could blame her for that.

She knew nothing about me and Dell, and though he hadn't been there in a while, I was still afraid that he might have left something that would make her suspicious.

There was nothing I could do about it now. Holly had been there and gone. There was no use getting angry at my landlady, who had just been trying to help.

"That's fine," I said. "You did the right thing. Thanks."

I walked up stairs as if danger awaited me, as if an unpleasant surprise lurked in my apartment. But why should I think that? Holly and I were still friends. We hadn't argued, or had a falling-out, or anything like that.

———

Nothing was out of order. My books, my papers, my coffee cup from this morning, everything was exactly where I'd left it. Nothing had been moved, nothing disturbed.

What had Holly done here? Did she just want a moment of quiet, a place to rest and escape from something? The bathroom? Mrs. O'Neal had said she'd only stayed a few minutes.

There was no sign that anyone had been in the bathroom.

It was only when I went into the bedroom that I noticed:

A blood red tulip lay crosswise across the bed.

A vampire tulip.

Holly was sending me a message.

That is, a message from Dell.

No one else knew about his vampire tulips—or did they?

A message from them both.

Had Dell dumped me for Holly? Were *they* together now? Was that what she was trying to tell me? Or was she just letting me know she'd found out about us, that she knew.

I was so upset and distracted that only now did I realize that Pyewacket hadn't trotted out to greet me when I came home.

Pyewacket!

I called him. No answer.

Was he all right? Had Holly let him out by mistake? He would never run away like that. Or would he? You never knew how much of the wild animal still lived inside the house cat.

I raced around the apartment, calling his name, looking under the bed, crawling under the table. Finally I heard a soft mewing from my bedroom closet.

I scrabbled under the tangle of sandals, boots, the nest of clothes that had slipped from their hangers onto the closet floor.

Finally I touched fur.

Pyewacket.

Thank God. I could breathe again.

But why was he in the closet? He'd never hid like that. Had Holly done something to scare him? Was he frightened because she'd been here without me? Was he afraid that something had happened to me?

He bit me. He hissed and bit me again as I gently dragged him out from the depths of the closet. Not hard, but he bit me, just the sting of teeth.

I yelped, more from shock than pain.

Pyewacket had never bitten me before.

Pyewacket jumped out of my hands and scooted across my bedroom. Hunched in the corner, he watched me from across the room.

Pyewacket hissed at me again.

I was shocked. It made no sense.

Was he sick?

I got as close as I could, as close as he let me.

It was almost as if he wanted me to see him up close. To see that he wasn't Pyewacket.

The cat looked a lot like Pyewacket. Slight, ginger-colored, with an intelligent face. A male. Black markings on his cheeks.

But he wasn't my cat.

He wasn't.

I sank to the floor, then got up again. I was afraid to be on the floor with a cat I'd never seen. How did I know he was friendly? I knew nothing about him. All I knew was that something mysterious and terrifying had happened.

———

I poured a saucer of milk, and the cat lapped it up. I decided to try a test. At the back of my pantry closet was a can of fancy cat food. Buy one, get one free. Pyewacket refused to touch it. I couldn't bring myself to throw out the unopened can. I hated waste, and maybe—doomsday scenario!—it would be the only food we had, and my cat would have to eat it.

Fake Cat emptied the food bowl within minutes and licked the sides of the dish with his long pink tongue.

Not Pyewacket.

Fake Cat.

Where had he come from?

Oh, Pyewacket! What happened to you? Where were you?

Who was this strange cat in my apartment?

I prayed without knowing what I was praying to. *Please bring Pyewacket back.*

I had to calm down. I called Holly. Her phone rang and rang. Her answering machine was off. I didn't want to seem like a stalker, so I waited fifteen minutes before I called again. No answer.

No answer.

No answer.

Chapter Seventeen

ANYONE WHO has ever lost a pet will know the grief I felt. By *lost* I don't mean died, with its terrible finality. Nor do I mean *wandered off*, which might make you think that your pet wanted to be free. This was different: uncertainty, torture, and misery, my spirits lifted and crashed by inklings of desperate hope. Was that Pyewacket mewing outside my door? He'd found his way home! You always saw news stories about cats left behind by accident during a long-distance move and traveling hundreds of miles to find their owners.

This calmed me for a moment, until the terror returned. Whatever I'd felt after losing Dell was nothing—nothing!—compared to this. Pyewacket. I whispered his name over and over, like a magic incantation that could bring him back.

This would turn out to be a bad dream. Everything would be like it was. He would jump up into bed beside me. We'd be together. Like before.

———

That was when I *really* discovered the friendship of alcohol. I'd been drinking maybe a little too heavily earlier, but now it was something I *needed*. Dell had left behind a bottle of bourbon. Sometimes the two of us would pass it back and forth, taking little nips.

The thought of Dell no longer hurt compared to my anguish about my cat. I just wanted not to feel anything. To be numb. Better yet, to be unconscious.

I gulped down the rest of the bottle.

I woke up at one in the morning with a raging headache.

Something was wrong. I remembered. I got out of bed. I went into the living room.

A ginger cat sat on my sofa. In the dark. When I turned on the light it gave me a furious look.

It snarled at me.

I had to stay calm. I had to work out a way to live with a cat that wasn't my cat. A cat that didn't want to be my cat, and I didn't want it, either.

I phoned Holly again. Where was she? With Dell. Of course. The tulip was a sign.

Did I need it spelled out for me that she was sleeping with Mr. Vampire Tulip? Holly and I had grown further apart than I'd realized—or admitted.

But that didn't explain why Pyewacket was gone and Fake Cat was here in his place!

Nothing explained that.

I got back into bed and tried another experiment. I made the little cooing noises that had always brought Pyewacket running in from wherever he was. Fake Cat refused to jump onto my bed. Fine. I didn't *want* a strange cat in my bed. He could claw me in my sleep. He seemed more skittish than aggressive, but how could I be sure?

It made no sense. Who would go to the trouble of switching someone's pet with a look-alike? It sounded like a bad dream.

———

The only possible explanation was that Holly and Dell were in this together. He had mind-controlled her into taking my cat and leaving another. Was this some evil psychology experiment? How does the research subject respond when her cat is kidnapped and switched?

Professor Muller's face floated before me like one of those hologram ghosts on haunted house rides in Disney World and places like that. Not that I've ever been there.

I didn't sleep all night. I kept thinking I could hear Fake Cat pacing the apartment, though everyone knows how quiet cats are.

I kept thinking I heard Pyewacket crying. But I was the one crying myself awake.

My impulse was to throw the vampire tulip in the garbage. But I kept it as evidence. Evidence of what? Someone had invaded my home and traded my cat for a strange cat. Why would anyone do that? Who would even believe that it had happened?

What was Holly's role in all this? I asked Mrs. O'Neal if Holly had been alone when she'd gone into my apartment.

"I wouldn't allow anything else. No funny business. I watched out to make sure."

"Did she have a cat with her?"

"A cat? Not hardly. A backpack, I remember. Quite a large

one. But not a cat. Certainly not. She was here to pick up a term paper."

The term paper that didn't exist. But maybe the cat in the backpack did. Arrive with one cat, swap it out, leave with another. Had she drugged Pyewacket and Fake Cat to get them into her backpack?

Pyewacket would never leave on his own. He would never do that. I knew him.

The tulip was a sign. Maybe Dell had told Holly everything. Every detail of our . . . But why would he? To control her. To make her feel that she had to prove she was tougher than me, the improvement on a lover (me) whom Dell swore he'd never loved.

Still . . . why would they conspire to steal my cat? What had I done to deserve *that*?

I kept thinking it had something to do with the psych department.

Was Dell experimenting on me? Was Holly his new assistant?

Maybe I was the subject for Dell's next research paper: How does an experimental subject behave when her cat is replaced by a stranger?

Who would publish a paper like that? Lots of journals, I imagined. The story could go beyond academia. Hollywood might come calling.

My mind was running away with me as I watched the clock hands stutter in the darkness.

———

I called Holly again at eight a.m., and this time she picked up. She sounded groggy.

I needed to sound normal. Reasonable. Not hysterical. Given what I had to say, it seemed important to seem . . . sane.

I said, "Holly, my God, I feel like we haven't talked in a million years."

"A million," she repeated sleepily.

"How are you?"

"Tired. Fine. What's up?"

I paused. "Mrs. O'Neal said you stopped by yesterday when I wasn't home."

"Oh, right. I meant to call you today and thank you. It was an emergency. I was desperate to pee. I was on my way to work"— Holly worked part-time at the supermarket near my apartment— "and I remembered that the toilet at work was broken. Again. Disgusting! There was no way I was going to make it through my shift. I was passing your place. You basically saved my life. Thank you. Like I said, I was going to call you today."

"Was Pyewacket here?"

"Of course. I gave him a little milk. We had a little cuddle. I've missed him, and I think he missed me."

I listened hard for an accusation. Was Holly reminding me how long it had been since I'd asked her to come visit? But no, it wasn't like that. She was just stating a fact.

"I didn't stay long. Your landlady had her ear to the door, and she wasn't moving till I left. I didn't hang around."

"I don't understand. I don't understand. I don't understand."

I seemed to have said it three times. "Did you leave a vampire tulip on my bed?"

"Did I what? A vampire *what*? Lorelei, are you okay? *What* don't you understand? What's wrong?"

"Did you steal Pyewacket and leave Fake Cat in his place?"

"I'm coming over," Holly said.

———

Years later, at the gala dinner, when I heard the women describe being saved by Holly, I remembered how I'd felt when she appeared that morning. I truly believed that she would help me. That she had come to save me.

She was there less than an hour after our phone call. Her hair was still wet from the shower. I suspected her of wanting me to see that she was shivering. Whatever. She was there.

Would a person who'd stolen my "boyfriend" and kidnapped my cat have been able to do that? Was Holly that good an actress? The answer, it turned out, was yes. But it's hard to believe that unless I factor in how stupid I must have been.

When Holly walked in, Fake Cat ran up to her—which he'd never done with me—and rubbed against her leg. Of course that made me suspicious. *Made* me suspicious? I was suspicious already.

She picked him up.

"Pyewacket," she murmured into Fake Cat's fur. "I've missed you!"

"It's not Pyewacket. It's Fake Cat."

"Lorelei. Talk to me! What's wrong?"

She'd gone pale. She looked like someone watching a friend have a breakdown and wondering how to get help.

But I wasn't crazy. I knew it.

She was acting. She was excellent. She knew what had happened.

I took her hand and pulled her into the bedroom. I waved the vampire tulip at her like I was shaking a cross at a vampire.

"Did you leave this here? What is this?"

"Oh, that. Geez, Lorelei. It's some kind of flower. I don't know. Some kind of tulip or something. I found it on the doormat outside your apartment door. I brought it in when I came."

"I asked if you'd brought a flower and left it in my room, and you didn't know."

"I had to pee. I was focused on that. I forgot about the flower."

She was lying. That wasn't just some kind of tulip. It had something to do with Dell. The only person who could have left it there was Dell, and Mrs. O'Neal would have told me if she'd let him into the building.

I don't have a doormat.

Holly said, "Lorelei, you're scaring me."

It's a terrible feeling, not to know the truth. Destabilizing. Maybe my mother was right: maybe I needed a psychiatrist. I could never be one. Because I didn't understand anyone. Not even my only friend, if Holly really was ever my friend.

I said, "Are you and Dell . . . ?"

"Me and who?" said Holly. Oh, she was good. Really good.

Maybe she was telling the truth about the tulip. But what about Pyewacket?

"I heard you were dating someone," I said.

"Who?"

I took a deep breath. "Professor Randall."

"Where did you hear that? Wow. I *wish*. The guy doesn't look at us. Not that way. Not any way. He wouldn't. He takes his job too seriously. He's professional. *A* professional."

Maybe she didn't know about me and Dell. Nothing else made sense.

"But I did meet this cool old Italian guy who's auditing my Freud and Leonardo course. Giorgio Serpenta. Strange name, huh?

I think he might be mega-rich. I think someone imagines he's going to give a bunch of money to the school. But I kind of like him . . ."

I said, "Please, Holly, I don't know what to do."

"About what, Lorelei?"

"About my cat."

"Oh, right. Pyewacket." Maybe she'd thought my delusion would go away if she ignored it. "Did you get any sleep? You look exhausted."

I hated it when people said that. Holly and I agreed on how much we hated it. Holly would never say that. Maybe this wasn't Holly, either; Fake Cat, Fake Holly. It was like *The Invasion of the Body Snatchers.* Your neighbor, your boyfriend, your mother have been replaced by pod people from outer space.

I had to get a grip. If I ever wanted to find Pyewacket again, I needed to get it together.

She said, "Do you want me to take Pyewacket for a few days? Until you sort things out. Do you think you might want to talk to someone?"

Talk to someone about the fact that my cat was not my cat?

The proof that I wasn't crazy was that I knew how crazy it sounded.

The vampire tulip was on my bed. My cat was gone, replaced by Fake Cat.

"Thanks," I told Holly. "Thanks for coming over. Let's talk soon. I'll call you."

———

I wanted to graduate. I wasn't about to go to counseling and telling an ambitious graduate student or depressed junior faculty member that someone had replaced my cat with a look-alike. Going to counseling at Woodward was always a risk. If you talked to someone, that person might later be watching you through a one-way mirror or, worse, might turn out to be your teaching assistant in a required course. So it was possible that your therapist would wind up grading your term papers.

There was no one I could tell. This was something that I had to work out on my own.

I vaguely recalled a comedy about a house-sitting couple that loses the homeowner's cat and tries to fool the owners by painting another cat to look like the lost one. But this wasn't that. This wasn't funny, and neither was that.

At the office supply mega store, I printed out one of the photos of Pyewacket that I'd taken on my phone. I ordered a hundred LOST CAT posters. It cost way more than I expected. I'd have to give up some luxuries—chocolate chip cookies, decent wine—but it was worth it. At least I was doing something. It made me feel less helpless.

I put up all the posters in one night, on telephone poles along Route 7, on lampposts on Main Street, on bulletin boards all over campus. I did it when no one would be around. I wasn't sure if it was legal or if I was defacing public property. I didn't feel like telling curious strangers about my situation. I didn't put my name on the poster, just my phone number, which gave me some privacy. Hardly anyone knew my number, so they'd have no way of knowing about Pyewacket and Fake Cat unless I told them. The only problem was that I'd had to include the line *Answers to Pyewacket*. Anyone who'd heard me mention his unusual name would probably remember.

A couple of people stopped to watch me, but no one said, "I'm sorry about your cat."

———

Fake Cat and I worked out a peaceful coexistence. We were room-mates. I fed him. I cleaned his litter box. We were like a divorced couple still living together, only we'd never been married.

Nothing changed my absolute certainty that he was not Pyewacket.

———

The next time I saw Holly was before Dell's class.

She'd caught up with me on the steps of the classroom build-ing. She asked if I was okay.

She looked flushed and rosy, and now that I think back, it seems to me that I was already watching Holly Snopes turn into Holly Serpenta. I couldn't see it then.

"Sure," I said. "I'm fine. I don't know what I was thinking. Me and Pyewacket have gotten it back together. I don't know what got into me. Some kind of PMS weirdness."

It hurt to lie to my so-called best friend under those desperate circumstances.

"Bullshit," said Holly.

It felt like a slap.

"I saw your poster," she said. "What is up with that? Please tell me you don't still think that Pyewacket has been switched and you're living with his double."

No one would believe that Fake Cat wasn't Pyewacket. Each day I woke up hoping it wasn't true, and each day I knew beyond any doubt that I was right.

"You need to talk to someone," she said. "Now."

All I could think of was the vampire tulip lying across my bed. The flower that Holly had put there.

"Why did you do it?" I said.

"Do what?" she said, then turned and went into the building.

———

The class always began with silence. The silence always felt different, depending on what each person was thinking.

One way we sometimes began was with someone saying what they'd been thinking in the silence. I only had one thought in my mind.

Pyewacket had been stolen. Fake Cat wasn't my cat.

Maybe I should talk about it. Maybe I should ask their help with my problem. But what if the problem was caused by our professor and one of our fellow students?

Finally, I was afraid of Dell. Afraid of Dell and Holly.

I was afraid of people thinking I'd gone crazy.

In the moments before class began, I distracted myself by trying to pick up some current between Holly and Dell. Professor Randall.

If something was going on, it was invisible. Why was I surprised? No one had suspected Dell and me. He was an expert at hiding. I must have learned from the master.

It felt strange, knowing Dell's nickname, when he was just Professor Randall again.

As always, there was a silence. But this one ended sooner.

Mitch said, "I saw your poster, Lorelei. That's awful about your cat. Have you found it yet?"

Holly was sitting to my left. Maybe I was imaging her lasering me with her eyes. If she hadn't been there, maybe I would have told them part of the truth. The part about the lost cat, not the part about the fake one. I would have accepted their sympathy for the person putting up posters about the loss of the love of her life.

Maybe I was afraid that Holly would tell if I didn't. Maybe I was afraid of hearing her say, *Lorelei thinks someone stole her cat and substituted a look-alike.* Maybe I was afraid to hear how it would sound if Holly said it. But why would she have said that if she was the one who did it? If it was all her fault? I wasn't thinking logically. I had forgotten what logic was.

We students knew a lot about one another. Secrets about our families, about sex and money and school. There had been laughter and shouts and tears. But now that I had something strange to tell them, I realized they knew nothing about me.

Twice a week, we'd been performing for one another and for Dell, who watched it all. Watched us. Took notes. Dell, who had brought me flowers and bourbon and taken me to the animal lab and to Thanksgiving dinner at the home of his sadistic boss. And then he had stopped sleeping with me and now, as far as I knew, was sleeping with my best friend and had kidnapped and switched my cat.

Does this sound unlikely? I know it does. But it happened.

Maybe Dell could have stayed in the background, stayed clean, hung it all on Holly. But the tulip was the tip-off. He wanted me to know that he was involved.

What had I done to deserve that? Of all the questions, that's the one least likely to get an answer. You can read the book of Job. Not even God can explain it.

We students were still performing for the invisible faces watching us from behind the one-way glass. Who was in there now? Had they seen my LOST CAT posters? Had they heard me talk about Pyewacket? I wish I'd never mentioned him. I should have kept him private.

It was good that people knew who he was. That they knew what he meant to me.

Maybe someone could help me.

I said, "A really strange thing happened. I don't understand it, and I know it's going to sound ridiculous or maybe crazy, but I swear it's true."

That got the class's attention. Professor Randall was making his snorting sound. Maybe he was worried. Worried that I might be setting off a string of firecrackers.

Professor Muller's Thanksgiving dinner played like a movie in my head.

The bad food. The boy who fainted and woke up to his father's insults.

The boy on the floor. The lecture about eugenics.

I saw Holly looking at me. Everyone was. The class was silent.

I said, "It's about my cat."

Mitch said, "It's lost. We know. We saw the signs. We're so sorry."

I expected an eye roll from some of the guys, no matter how they tried to control it. But they heard something in my voice.

I said, "Someone stole my cat."

That got a reaction. Who would do that? Everyone talking at once, though talking over each other was breaking one of the few rules we had in the class.

"And that person or persons, whoever they are, substituted another cat that looks just like my cat. But he isn't my cat."

It seemed as if they were all holding their breath until they figured out if I was serious.

I was serious. Deadly serious. Somebody laughed.

Drew said, "I saw a movie like that. The couple was supposed to house-sit a cat, but the cat ran away, so they got another cat and tried to make it look like the real cat but—"

"This isn't that," I said. "This isn't comedy. This is some psycho mind game that someone is playing on me."

I didn't look at Dell or at Holly. I couldn't even check to see if they were looking at me.

I'd kicked things up to another level.

Mitch said, "Lorelei? What do you mean, exactly?"

"It's a ginger cat. But not mine. Another ginger cat. Same size, maybe a little thinner. A similar face. A male. Black markings. Just not Pyewacket. A different cat. Someone came into my apartment and stole my cat and substituted another one."

Again I didn't look at Holly. The person I *should* have looked at. I didn't look at Dell. Professor Randall. I stared into the middle distance. Like a crazy person. I must have sounded insane. I probably looked insane, too.

Another laugh. I didn't blame them.

I hated them anyway. All of them. None of them believed me. None of them would help me. I was entirely alone.

There were some big talkers in that class, but even they were struck speechless when I—Lorelei, the pretty, rather quiet girl who lived alone with her cat—said that my cat wasn't my real cat.

Dell—Professor Randall—so rarely spoke that we were startled when he said, "How does Lorelei's story make the rest of you feel?"

If he was behind the kidnapping, his calm was especially chilling. He showed no emotion. He was facilitating a class.

How many people were watching behind the glass? What did *they* think about my story?

Matt said, "Can I be honest?"

A few students laughed. The class was all about honesty, right? The subject we kept coming back to.

"How does it *honestly* make me feel? Honestly, it makes me feel like Lorelei has lost her fucking mind."

"Totally batshit," said Drew.

He laughed, then everyone laughed. There was a silence.

Did the people behind the glass laugh too? Why did I care about them?

Professor Randall said, "That's not helpful for Lorelei. Or for your classmates. Not helpful at all."

Another silence.

I looked up. No one looked at me.

Silence. More silence.

They thought I was crazy. They thought I was making it up. They didn't know what to think, and they hated me for it.

They'd turned against others in the group. Now it was my turn.

It was awful. There were so many reasons to burst into tears that I couldn't let myself do it.

And that, strangely enough, was that. End of story. Discussion ended. No one said another word about my cat not being my cat.

The class went on to talk about a dream Jim had, a recurrent dream about a flood or something. The guys were always dreaming about floods.

Somehow I understood that no one would bring up my cat again. No one would ask me. It would not be mentioned.

Professor Randall said, "Anyone want to comment about something that happened today?"

No one wanted to comment. No one knew what to say.

Or maybe Matt had said it for all of them.

I was out of my fucking mind.

———

After class, Professor Randall asked me to come to his office.

I felt shaky. Now everything would be explained. Dell would tell me why he had left me, or maybe he'd say that he hadn't left me. Maybe we were just "taking a break" and he'd forgotten to tell me. He would explain how the red-black tulip came to be on my doorstep, on my bed, and solve the mystery of Pyewacket and Fake Cat.

He followed me out of the classroom. We walked down the hall to his office. I was so worried about bumping into him, I kept bumping into the wall.

There was no charge, no buzz between us. I felt like I was physically shrinking. By the time we got to his office, I was the size of a mouse.

Dell—Professor Randall—motioned for mouse-me to take the chair. He sat behind his desk. He didn't seem relaxed. He didn't seem nervous. He didn't seem anything.

He opened a notebook and reached for a pen.

He said, "Tell me, Lorelei, when did these thoughts about your cat begin?"

I said, "Someone left a vampire tulip on my bed. Any idea who that could be?" My voice sounded oddly squeaky. Just saying that had taken all my strength, and I slumped back, exhausted.

"A flower?'

"Not just any flower. A vampire tulip."

"Does that particular flower hold some special significance for you?"

Did that flower have some special significance for me? Was he joking? The flower he brought me the first time and every time after that when we were sleeping together?

I said, "You know what I'm talking about."

There. I'd said it. Let it all come down.

"I wish I did," he said. "Help me."

Help him? I really had gone insane. But wait.

This was textbook gaslighting. This was textbook *Rosemary's Baby*. Was this *Through the Looking Glass*? Was I Alice?

The pod people and their pod cats had taken over the living. Inhabited their bodies.

"You don't know?" I was stalling for time.

"Know *what*, Lorelei? What do you think I should know?" Not guilty, not accusing. Not upset. Absolutely toneless. Clinical. Robotic.

I couldn't speak. This wasn't counseling, or a teacher-student chat. It was an interview. An interrogation. What was his science experiment about? Jealousy? Sanity? Attachment? Humans and their pets? Grief and loss?

Mind Control? That was Professor Muller's passion. Maybe he had suggested or at least approved whatever this was. Whatever game Dell was playing.

"You don't know about the flower?"

"Know what about the flower?"

Another silence. I kept trying to think. But my thoughts kept unraveling, like they do at the edge of sleep.

"So when did these ideas start? This . . . ideation about your cat."

Ideation meant *not real*. But something real had happened.

He wasn't the same person.

Professor Randall. Not Dell.

"My cat" was all I could say.

He looked disappointed, not emotionally, more like a scientist not getting encouraging results. Was I always his research subject? Was his affection for Pyewacket part of the experiment? Had I imagined our love affair, the flower on my bed, and now Fake Cat not being my cat? He was older than me, a professor. How could I doubt his version of events? His version was: There *were* no events. Nothing to explain.

Something had thrown me off. Schizophrenia often began in people around my age.

I knew I wasn't crazy. I thought of all the books and films in which the crazy person (a woman, usually) keeps insisting she's sane.

He asked how I knew that Fake Cat wasn't Pyewacket. What exactly was different?

"The hissing," I said. "The biting. Everything."

I'd thought that he and Pyewacket were friends. Now he was acting as if he'd never met him. As if the only things he knew about my cat were what I'd said in class.

"And you're saying . . . this new cat looks just like him."

I sat there. I went along with it. We both pretended. We acted.

I said, "I know it's not Pyewacket. I know it. Everything about him is different. Every cell in his body."

Professor Randall looked simultaneously impatient and proud of himself for hiding his impatience with a hopeless case.

He said, "Thank you, Lorelei. Thanks for your time. Let's talk again soon, shall we?"

He got up.

It was time for me to go.

I stood. I actually thanked him. Thank you for everything.

I left.

I wanted to hang around outside his office, to see who went in. I wanted to follow him home. But I wasn't a stalker. Not yet.

Holly was the one I stalked.

Dell was the one who got away.

And even as I stalked Holly, someone was stalking me.

Chapter Eighteen

*A*FTER PYEWACKET was stolen, after I got it through my head that *someone would do something like that*, that my former best friend and ex-lover would do that to me, the energy just went out of me. Like air from a balloon. Not a puncture. Not an explosion.

A slow leak.

My parents had been right to trust my landlady. Mrs. O'Neal was the only one who noticed that I'd stopped leaving my apartment, quit taking out the cat box and the garbage. She probably had her ear to the pipes and knew I no longer bathed.

None of my teachers noticed when I stopped coming to class. Maybe Professor Randall asked if anyone knew where I was, but he never took it further, never came to check.

Maybe he never even asked. He marked me absent. Lorelei Green? Not here. Again.

Probably he was relieved that I was gone. I had no way of knowing.

My landlady was the only one who came to see about me. I opened my door and said I was fine. Thank you, Mrs. O'Neal. I sent her away.

Holly didn't come to find out what happened to me. I think I'd scared her. She had reason to be scared.

And yet I like to think that Holly was the one who called the department secretary. The one who told the school that someone had to go see about me, do something about me. The future Woman of the Year saved me, just as she would go on to save so many other women.

Maybe I was her first rescue; I was where she got the taste for it.

I was practice.

Do you get credit for saving someone if you created the situation they need to be saved from?

The department secretary called me at home. I answered. She said I'd been missing classes, not handing in papers. She asked if I wanted to "see someone," and when I said I didn't, she called my parents.

My parents came and got me just before the term ended. I'd been in bed for a while. I'd fed Fake Cat. But I wasn't eating.

My parents talked about my being back at school soon, maybe by the start of the second semester. But I knew I was leaving for good. I packed up my apartment and loaded Fake Cat into a carrying cage.

My mother must have been so worried, she "forgot" about Thanksgiving, when, just to be nasty, she'd pretended Dad had respiratory problems and couldn't have a cat in the house.

Her lie had started the trouble. No wonder I was upset. Everyone was gaslighting me. Everywhere I looked.

Fake Cat and I got into the back of my parents' car. I didn't turn around as we left. I didn't look back at Mrs. O'Neal. I watched her wave in my dad's rearview mirror. Her face was happy and sad. My parents had forfeited two months' rent and the security deposit.

My mother's low estimation of me was confirmed. My dad's main concern was if they get a pro-rated refund for the months I'd dropped out.

I moved back into my childhood bedroom with Fake Cat. I didn't tell my parents I called him Fake Cat, that he wasn't Pyewacket. I called him Pyewacket when they were around him, which wasn't very often.

They didn't seem to notice.

Only once, my mother said, "I don't think your cat liked going away to school all that much. He's grumpier and more skittish even than last summer."

She'd seen through Fake Cat's disguise!

I almost broke down and told her. But I knew it wouldn't go well. Where would I begin? And maybe she was just being critical. Not drawing any conclusions.

I never bonded with Fake Cat. It wasn't his fault. He was a perfectly decent cat. He just wasn't Pyewacket, and I couldn't forgive him for it. He was the only cat I ever had that I didn't love. Poor thing. I never blamed him. I knew he'd been stolen from somewhere, which should have touched my heart, but all I could see was what he wasn't. I admit it. I let Fake Cat down.

One night my dad came home late. He'd been drinking, and he forgot to close the front door. Fake Cat slipped past him, ran off, and never came home.

I guess that Fake Cat hadn't bonded with me, either. His getting lost was a good excuse for me to be angry at my father. But the truth was, I was relieved.

It was what I always worried would happen with Pyewacket that school year he stayed with my parents. But Pyewacket would never have run away.

Fake Cat would. And he did.

I didn't get another cat till I moved out again and was living on my own. Then I had Flora, then Simone.

Now I have Catzilla. I've always tried to find a name that fit my cat's personality. So that should tell you something about my monster cat.

Catzilla was the one to whom I would tell all the details of my dinner with the Woman of the Year. Catzilla would understand.

People who say that you and your cat can't share jokes know nothing about cats. Cats have a sense of humor. Anyway, some of them do. When I told him about my evening, Catzilla would laugh in all the right places.

I have never been interested in the competition between dog people and cat people. Cats rule, Dogs drool. That sort of thing. Some dogs and cats hate each other, some people hate one or the other, but dogs and cats are not a popularity contest; no one is making you vote.

Lately, what has worried me most was a newspaper article I read about how closely the cat genome resembles its human equivalent. More so than the mouse or the dog. Better experimental subjects. I don't like how that sounds.

You can see, with my history, why I would be upset by any suggestion of animal experimentation, though the article made a point of the fact that no animals would be hurt. The researchers would only have to draw a small amount of the animal's blood.

Chapter Nineteen

*I*T WAS not a personal high point. Back home, living with my parents, who still called me Laura Lee, as if college had been a dream and I was never Lorelei.

I was unemployed and living at home with a strange cat I couldn't bond with. It let me feed it. It lived in my room. It shit and peed in its box. We left each other alone.

A hard spring, a harder summer. I began to think that my mother was right about me. About my dreams of a future that was never going to happen.

Best case: I had an overactive imagination. I'd imagined that someone had swapped my cat for a stranger. I'd imagined that I'd had a love affair with my teacher. I'd imagined that someone had left a blood-red tulip on my bed, and that my former best friend was conspiring against me with my former lover.

Worst case: I was insane.

I might have thought I'd made it all up—except for a terrible thing that happened.

———

It was August. The weather was hot. Even the birds outside my window were too tired and sweaty to sing. My mother knocked on my door.

"You got a letter," she said. "A package. Addressed to Lorelei Green. Whoever that is, Laura Lee. I'm leaving it out here." The last time she'd come into my room, I'd yelled at her until she backed out. A different mother would have raised a different daughter who wouldn't wind up like this. Do I sound like Professor Muller? Was I accusing my mother of conditioning me to be a disaster?

I thought about the professor's children. That sad girl, the boy who fainted. Starved into speaking in sentences. The boy terrorized and insulted. What would happen to them? Many people had worse childhoods than mine. I would rather be me, Lorelei Green, than one of Professor Muller's kids. I knew that was setting the bar pretty low.

A package? I'd gotten several letters from the college, telling me how many credits I had, how many I needed to graduate, asking me how long a leave of absence I planned to take, giving directions for reapplying.

An eight-by-eleven manila envelope. Addressed to Lorelei Green. No return address.

The handwriting was unfamiliar.

I opened it.

Inside were two photographs. Both taken in the same place.

The animal lab. I recognized it. A sink, a metal table.

Only one cage.

Where were the monkeys?

It took me a beat to be sure I was seeing what I thought.

Something I prayed I *wasn't* seeing.

In the photo was a cat. In a cage.

The second photo was a close-up.

I knew what I was going to see.

Pyewacket was wearing a helmet hooked up to a wire.

Nothing worse had ever happened to me. Nothing worse has happened since.

I can close my eyes and see it now. I try not to. And mostly I succeed.

My feet melted into the rubbery ground. I heard myself howl. Someone else was doing a bad ambulance imitation.

I felt what Pyewacket was feeling. The panic, helplessness, pain, and fear. The loneliness and confusion. The being I loved best in the world was being imprisoned and tormented.

I screamed, or anyway tried to. I heard myself making gibbering moans, like the sounds I hear myself make waking from a nightmare. I remember sliding to the ground. I guess I must have blacked out. Just before the world went glittery then dark, I thought of the boy fainting that Thanksgiving.

I woke up with my mother pushing and pulling me into bed. I fell asleep and didn't wake up until the next morning.

The photos were gone. My mother must have seen them and understood and taken them away so I wouldn't see them again.

I didn't want to ask my mother what she'd done with them. I didn't want to ask if now she understood what had happened. If she put it all together—that Fake Cat wasn't Pyewacket. That Pyewacket was in a lab.

We never spoke about it. How insane is that? Your daughter gets photos of her cat being tortured.

She faints dead away.

Of course you look at the photos.

And you never discuss it.

———

I never knew what the photos were intended to do. Destroy me, I imagine. Finish me off. But they did the opposite. It worked on me like a treatment with no recovery time. It shocked me into action. It could have gone the opposite way. I'm grateful that it didn't.

I spent a day searching the web for stories about cats used in lab experiments. I couldn't find any, which probably meant that no one was admitting it. It wasn't till years later that I read about cats' genomes being so much like humans'.

The next day, I got up and showered and brushed my hair. I emptied my checking account and bought a round-trip ticket to Great Barrington.

I left at dawn and arrived just as Professor Muller's Intro to Psych class was letting out. I went up to him after class. He shrank back, as if someone calling his name was a physical attack.

He was wearing his eye patch. He looked like an actor from a 1940s horror movie.

I said, "I'm Lorelei Green."

He peered at me through his one good eye.

"Thanksgiving," he said blankly.

"Exactly. But that's not why I'm here. I have on good information that there are some . . . concerns about your animal lab. I have been asked by a national publication to . . ."

Profess Muller's face stiffened. "Are you from PETA? Or some other crackpot organization? Do you know how many medical advances have been made because of animal research? So what exactly have you heard?"

"I'm not at liberty to disclose that."

Professor Muller looked harder at me. I could see pieces snap together behind his one terrifying eye. Something had set off alarm bells. What *was* he doing in that lab? Something that bothered him enough that even I—a liar, a nobody—could see it on his face? Or maybe he was just getting old, slipping. Disconnected. Anything was possible. I had no way of knowing.

All at once I felt time-transported back to how I'd felt in his house, that Thanksgiving, when I'd felt so shockingly cold, and what I imagined the boy was feeling. Meanwhile the professor fixed me with his horror-film one eye.

I heard my voice, from a distance. "One report claims that you are using cats in animal research."

"Cats! What serious scientist would use cats? And what if we are? Fascinating, in their own way. But not useful for our purposes. They're hard to control, you've no doubt heard the expression *herding cats*. One can hardly teach them anything interesting at all, though I gather there exists videos pretending they play the piano. So no, if that is your question, the answer is no. We have no cats in our laboratory. We have never had cats in our lab."

He was wrong. You can teach cats lots of things. I'd taught Pyewacket so much. It seemed like bad luck to think about Pyewacket. But I was doing this for him.

A new expression crossed the professor's craggy face, a twitch of a smile in which I saw . . . what? Satisfaction? Amusement? What if he and Dell *were* in this together? What if they'd dreamed up this experiment and were monitoring my reactions. I was being paranoid. But I'd seen the photos. Someone meant me to see them.

"I have an idea," the professor said. "Why don't you and I take a little tour of the lab? You can see that there's nothing untoward, none of whatever Gothic cruelties you have been imagining. Then we can bid each other good day and be on our merry way."

Our merry way. He was tormenting me. Playing with me. And I could do nothing.

I never expected this. I imagined he'd try to prevent my seeing the lab where Pyewacket was being held.

I had to pretend that I'd never been there before. Or did he know that Dell had taken me? How much did he know? It frightened me, not knowing.

Fear was part of the test I had to pass. Be cool. Be smart. Be steady. Pyewacket's life might be at stake.

I decided to say nothing. To show no reaction. To find my cat.

I recognized the smell and the lighting. Fetid. Scary. Awful. Even so, I couldn't help feeling a little nostalgic. Dell had taken me there when I still thought he loved me. It was the last place we'd been together—not counting Professor Muller's Thanksgiving dinner.

The fluorescent light buzzed, like before. I heard water dripping and rodents scurrying over metal and sand. There were Abba and Babba. Napping in their cages. I didn't look at them. It hurt to remember Dell waking them with Beethoven. For a moment, I thought about trying it. A bad idea, in every way.

"No cats," said Professor Muller. "See for yourself, young lady."

I walked up and down the aisles. Lab equipment, mice. The monkeys. He was right. No cats.

No Pyewacket.

"Someone stole my cat," I said. "And replaced him with a lookalike. And they had him here, in a cage, in your lab."

The professor's skin looked greenish in the sickly light, and he leaned in close enough for me to see every pucker in the scar down his cheek.

"Clearly, you are under some strain. Delusions are the sort of thing for which my professional colleagues—some of them—can be helpful. If you call my secretary, she can give you some names of doctors in the area."

"I'm not in the area." I knew I would get nothing from him. The truth? What had I been thinking? I turned and walked out of the lab. Only when I got outside did I realize how violently I was trembling.

The professor had made his son faint. What else could he do? No wonder I was scared of him. He was someone to fear.

———

I took the next bus home. That same week I went out and got a job as a receptionist at Cobrox. I was still pretty enough for an office to want me as their public face.

Already I wasn't as pretty as I had been just a few months before. Maybe I was the only one who saw the difference when I looked in the mirror. Things had taken a downturn after Pyewacket was stolen and I left college. I no longer looked like Catherine Deneuve playing a rich, bored French whore. I looked (at least to myself) like a Depression-era mom fending off the bank.

By that fall, I'd moved out of my parents' house. I'd found the sweet little rent-controlled walk-up in Brooklyn Heights. Modest, but it was home. I loved it. It had a skylight, so I could have plants. I had two small Persian rugs, bookshelves, and some paintings. The fireplace was nonfunctional, but it made the place feel like home. When you lived in a place for a long time, it knew you, and you knew it.

After I'd "gotten over" Pyewacket, I adopted another cat— Flora, who was part Siamese, part tabby—from a shelter on the

Lower East Side. I made sure Flora never knew I could never love her as much as I'd loved Pyewacket. I loved her just as I loved them all. But your first is always your first. I sometimes wonder if Catzilla has finally taken Pyewacket's place.

Are you surprised that I'm angry? No gory crime scene photo could be worse than the image of Pyewacket hooked up to the electrodes.

Why am I telling you this? Why am I doing this to you?

I'll float that word again: *revenge.* You want to prove that someone deserved what you did later.

Holly's punishment—the poisoning—wasn't half as bad as her crime.

She hadn't suffered as much as I did.

Or so I thought at the time.

I have tried, really tried, not to dwell on the past. But the past won't let you forget it.

Every so often I'd see Holly's name in the news. First she turned up in photos of society parties. I'd wonder, *Why is Holly getting her picture taken with the mayor of New York?* After a while I got used to it. Though to be honest, the articles about her activism and her charitable work all over the globe could put me in a bad mood for days.

There was sympathetic press coverage and a Twitter outpouring when her husband died. Several shelter magazines ran stories about her recuperating on her husband's Tuscan estate, along with her two beautiful, photogenic, bilingual children. Both children followed in their mother's footsteps. Both married young, both married rich Italians and were living in their spouses' ancestral palazzi, one in Venice, one in Milan.

Holly passed in and out of the spotlight. She was never out of it for very long, and each return brought fresh reports of the miracles she'd worked since her fans had caught up with her last. Just when I thought that the world was done with Holly, the light would find her again.

The latest was the knife in my heart. The cover story in the Woodward College alumni magazine.

There Holly was, looking at me through the plastic cover. Inside, along with photographs of Holly in her West Village town house, her beach house in Amagansett, and her first husband's family Tuscan villa, was a story about her global empire of good deeds.

Frankly, I was surprised to see her in the college magazine. Her #MeToo moment must have caused some embarrassment for the school. But that was over. Forgotten. And Holly was famous. A celebrity graduate.

The (male) writer had fallen in love with Holly, Woodward's very own good-works media star. He grieved with her over the husbands and listened in awe as she told some of the stories about the refugee camp and the chess club that I would hear her tell again at the gala dinner.

So it wasn't true that the Woman of the Year dinner was the first thing that kicked up my—let's say—*negative* feelings about Holly. Our college alumni magazine started something simmering that, a few months later, ignited when I got the email saying that Holly was the Woman of the Year.

Anyone who followed Holly's career knew there were some things the article left out. The article didn't mention her #MeToo accusation. It didn't mention Professor Randall or the psych department or the animal labs.

The point was that Holly went to Woodward. The point was all the famous and wonderful things she had done since she graduated. The point was the college's student application rate and potential donors.

———

The swell of popularity that culminated in Holly's coronation began at the time when women were coming forward with their stories.

Of course I cheered (silently) each time a woman spoke up about harassment and abuse.

Each time I read one of these brave declarations, I told Catzilla how important it was. How personal for me. I like to think that my cat understood, even though he was a boy.

I would never know who I could have become in life without the harm I suffered from that psych class. And from my professor. And from what happened with my cat.

I wanted to tell my story. But who would listen? I wasn't a movie star assaulted by a powerful producer. Who cared about a former college girl, now middle-aged, who, twenty years ago, slept with her college professor and lost her cat?

Dell was still teaching at Woodward. Professor Muller was now professor emeritus. He still published papers that appeared in journals and online, beyond a steep paywall.

———

Of course Holly had *her* story.

Holly knew how to catch a wave. She had the luxury surfboard. The rest of us, the unlucky ones, were paddling to shore with our hands.

I shouldn't have resented her. I should have been delighted that she accused my abuser.

She spoke out against the person I would have accused if anyone would have listened to me. But it bothered me that *she* got to tell the story.

This time it wasn't just envy.

It bothered me more that she left out the worst part: what the two of them did to me.

She left out the part about my cat. How could I forgive her?

I've tried not to think about Holly and Dell. And Pyewacket. But I've thought about them a lot. Does having someone's name on Google Alert mean you are their stalker?

Holly was too famous to stop being famous unless she did something terrible. Or died, though that could make her *more* famous. For a while.

She'd done good things. She'd helped women. She was the Woman of the Year.

Each of us has someone we think is richer and more famous than that person deserves.

I cut out Holly's #MeToo statement from the newspaper. I still have the clipping somewhere. Or maybe I'm misremembering. Maybe it's a printout from my computer. I know where to find it, but I don't need to look.

I've reread it so many times I know it pretty much by heart.

HOLLY SERPENTA ACCUSES PSYCH PROFESSOR IN
COLLEGE HARASSMENT CLAIM

My Story by Holly Serpenta

My story is so much less painful than what so many women have suffered. I almost hesitate to add it to the growing number of gut-wrenching accounts of violence, cruelty, and intimidation.

Gut-wrenching? I could never be friends with someone who said *gut-wrenching*. Maybe someone wrote it for her. One of her assistants. Certainly someone edited it, with her collaboration.

I know that my readers, my fans, my loyal supporters will assume that I have totally recovered from what happened twenty years ago. I don't mean to sound boastful when I say I know what the public must think: if anyone has moved on, if anyone has grown past trauma, Holly Serpenta has.

But we never lose the memory. The shame. It never goes away. Some nights I dream about it. That experience marked me.

My abuser ruined my life. Or anyway, for a while.

Hard work, a sense of purpose, and my children got me through. I know I have been luckier than so many other women. My work has been to make it so that women don't need to depend on luck.

Our stories need to be told.

So here goes:

When I was in college, John James "Dell" Randall, my psychology professor at Woodward University, pressured me into having a sexual affair. If I wanted to pass his course and graduate from college, I had to sleep with him. He knew, from things I had said in class, that my parents couldn't afford another term. If I didn't graduate that spring, I never would.

Like all predators, he went for the vulnerable ones. My working-class background made me an outlier in college.

This man was a psychologist, entrusted with the education of the young. His course was almost like group therapy. So he knew more about us than most professors did. He knew our weak spots, fears, dreams, vanities. And all the time he was

sitting there, listening to us, he was plotting to use that knowledge against young women.

He chose to focus on me.

I'd had to put the newspaper down. He'd chosen to focus on
Holly? He slept with me, Lorelei, for six weeks. Where was I in
this story?

It was infuriating and painful, even though I was glad that
Holly was doing this at all. So what if she hadn't mentioned me.
She was blowing the whistle on him.

I don't know how many other students Professor Randall
harmed over his long career. But I don't imagine he stopped
with me.

Predators never stop until someone stops them.

I hope that this will stop him—at last. My harasser is still
teaching. He's published books on psychological experimentation, and also one that was quite popular. The most recent is *The
History of Mind Control, from the Inquisition to the iPhone.*

His behavior was friendly at first. Professional. Collegial.
Then it got more inappropriate, and finally romantic. He always
made the first move.

He was always the aggressor.

I was young. I was his student. I was overwhelmed.

He had all the power.

By the time he brought me flowers, I knew where we were
headed.

What did Holly mean by *flowers*? What flower did she
mean? A red tulip? Wouldn't that have been a good detail to

make her story more poignant? To make it sadder and more convincing?

Or maybe I was the only one who would have paid attention to that. Dell and I would have noticed.

When Holly's statement first appeared, he was still teaching at Woodward.

It felt strange reading something that I knew Dell had read. It reminded me that our connection would never totally go away.

I returned to Holly's essay.

> One thing led to another. I'm not proud of what I did. I was young. I was being…not exactly abused, but definitely taken advantage of.
>
> The night our affair ended, he took me to see the disgusting animal laboratory they had at our school. This vile institution tormented monkeys and dogs and mice.

Cats, I thought. She didn't mention cats. She didn't want to remember.

> My abuser told me that they were teaching the monkeys their colors. When they heard the word *red*, they were supposed to press the red lever. They got an electric shock when they made a mistake. The department paid students to shock them. Professor Randall thought that it was a good thing. He thought that it was science. Oh, those poor helpless creatures!

I'm sure that Holly meant for her #MeToo statement to help other women and to stop men like Dell. In fact, she'd meant to stop the same harasser who had harassed me. But I read it as a personal attack. Even after what they did to Pyewacket, I hated that Dell took Holly to the animal lab. Nothing is more humiliating than finding out that our lover did the exact same things with another person.

Control was their subject. Dell and Professor Muller.

Even though it was painful, I made myself picture the photo of Pyewacket. The wire. The metal helmet squeezing his beautiful head.

Holly's statement went on.

> At our school, there was an animal cruelty ring masquerading as science. I know that I should have stopped it. I should have been the whistleblower. I should have told the authorities.
>
> Except that my professors *were* the authorities. I felt so small and powerless against the men (of course they were men) who would do something like that.
>
> But I didn't . . . I didn't tell anyone. Who would I tell?
>
> This professor, my abuser, he was part of it. A harasser and a sadist. He was untouchable. They did things you could never do now, though maybe they're still doing it.
>
> When I tried to end our relationship, he ruined my future as a psychologist.
>
> That had been my dream. That was why I went to that school. I wanted to help people. I wanted to use my power to help other women. I still do.
>
> He pulled strings. Wrote letters. He made sure I had no future, no dream.
>
> Or anyway, he tried. He told me he didn't care about me. He told me he never had cared about me.

But now he said that he couldn't trust me. I knew too much about what went on at that school. He needed to obliterate me. To make me a nonperson.

He carried out his threat. I couldn't get into a graduate program. I had perfect grades. A 4.0 average. Except for his course. He failed me. Probably that was enough.

I won't lie. I cried for a year. I lived with my parents and worked as a supermarket checker in Iowa. Then I went to Europe and got into human rights and came home and started over at Columbia.

The rest, as they say, is history.

In a way I'm grateful, because my life has turned out better than if he'd helped me. But I hate to think that he's been at that school for twenty more years. He must have abused other girls. Everyone has been silent, just like we were silent about the animal labs.

Do people need to be stopped from hurting themselves? We need to respect their right to self-determination, even when we think we know what would be good for them.

Together, we women are more powerful than our individual selves. Especially now at this time when women everywhere are finally being heard.

A new day is dawning. We believe women. Time's Up.

Your sister in struggle,
Holly Serpenta

If I had to pick the most offensive sentence from Holly's steaming pile of a statement it would be: *I won't lie.* And if had to pick the part that upset me most it would be that little paragraph near the end, about intervening to keep people from hurting themselves.

The passage doesn't connect to anything else in the story. What disturbed me was that it was a quote from a paper that Professor Randall published in the *New York Journal of Abnormal Psychology*, ten years after we knew him, ten years before Holly accused him.

She quoted from his article when she ruined his life. She must have been really angry.

Chapter Twenty

*D*ELL'S PAPER was entitled: "Dissociative Behavior, Romantic Delusion, and Transferential Control: An Observational Case Study."

For all my pretending to let go of the past, I'd reread Dell's paper so often that Holly's quote from it jumped right out.

Was it a joke she was making? Was it a signal between them?

I don't know why it made me more certain that, no matter what Holly was saying, the two of them had been in it together. For scientific reasons. They had plotted against me.

———

Holly had written me out of the story. What Dell had done to me, what they both had done to me, was never mentioned. What if Holly's #MeToo statement included the truth about what she and Dell did to my cat? There was nothing in any of the stories or news items or video clips that followed in the wake of Holly's statement—no mention of Pyewacket or Fake Cat or the vampire tulips.

Fake Cat was not Pyewacket, and Holly knew it. What they'd done was weird and cruel, and Holly knew that too.

Stealing your friend's cat and swapping it for a fake one and gaslighting your friend and fucking her boyfriend and sending her pictures of her cat caged and tortured in an animal lab—or even just conspiring with someone who did that—was not the kind of detail that Holly wanted to include in her righteous #MeToo statement. How would her fans like *that*?

———

This is what I read in a newspaper article that appeared not long after Holly's statement:

> In the wake of Holly Serpenta's #MeToo accusations, which have been supported by several other women who wish to remain anonymous, Professor Randall has been encouraged to take early retirement. His teaching responsibilities have been suspended.

———

I wish I were more organized. Somewhere buried among my books and papers is an item containing a few lines about Dell's death in a climbing accident in the hills above Oaxaca.

Oh, and there's another little item, a video clip from a local TV station reporting on a mass demonstration against a testing facility that, believe it or not, still existed at Woodward College at the time Holly published her essay. According to the reporter, it had been operating in secret until Holly Serpenta's #MeToo exposé prompted a thorough investigation. A hunger strike followed, an agreement was reached, and the lab was shut down.

———

It was around the time of Holly's #MeToo accusation that I began—just began—to wonder if there wasn't something that could be done, some fitting nonfatal revenge I could take. Nothing close to a punch in the face, more like a little bitch slap. Something to make me feel more cheerful about the whole situation.

I'm not a vengeful person, not a grudge holder. But anyone can get pushed too far. Holly's saying she owed Dell something—that her life turned out *better* because of him—was sort of like me thanking Strep Throat Dad rapist because he led me to Pyewacket.

Not to be competitive, but my life had turned out worse.

I owed Dell nothing. Nothing. Holly owed me everything.

And I believed she should pay.

Chapter Twenty-One

YEARS AGO, as soon as I figured out how to google someone, I googled Dell.

The most interesting thing I found was the paper that John James Randall, Professor of Psychology, Woodward University, wrote for the *New York Journal of Abnormal Psychology*.

I had to pay thirty-five dollars to get it from behind the paywall. This was when everyone was still saying that the web should be free. Thirty-five dollars was serious money to me, but I "bought" the article, because I had an inkling of what it contained.

It crossed my mind that Dell—Professor Randall—was trying something similar to what Oliver Sacks had done in his popular essays about unusual neurological conditions. That's why—now that I am able to think of it without fury or pain—I noticed that his article sounded less scholarly, more like something written for a more general audience, though with one foot still in academia, to be safe.

The title looked quite comfortable in the journal's table of contents. "Dissociative Behavior, Romantic Delusion, and Transferent Control: An Observational Case Study."

But the text of the paper was a little less jargon-ridden.

A college undergraduate, Miss L, 21, came in for counseling after experiencing a disturbance in her perception of reality.

For some time she had been under the delusion that she and one of her professors were engaged in a torrid love affair.

She may sound like the sort of patient who would have seen Freud, the sort of patient whom Freud would have misdiagnosed and mistreated. But this was one of those cases in which—for reasons that would become clear later—the patient's condition was more complicated, stranger, and more interesting than what used to be diagnosed, by our man from Vienna, as female hysteria.

No one else, not her friends or her "lover," believed that this affair was occurring or had ever occurred.

Her friends and classmates noticed her growing distance from reality, especially because she had convinced herself that it was necessary to keep this "love affair" a secret. Finally her best friend convinced her to seek counseling with me.

A stone of sick, cold dread was already weighing in my stomach as I read on:

The young woman who came into my office had a look I would describe, perhaps unprofessionally, as haunted. *She was pretty, but hers was the kind of beauty that so often fades before its time.*

We met for eight to ten sessions, each for about fifty-five minutes. She didn't seem suicidal, which is always our main concern. I encouraged her to call me in emergencies. I gave her my card.

Professor Randall never gave me his card. I don't believe he had a card.

But she never took me up on my invitation, though I believe she should have.

During our sessions I took copious notes.

She asked why I was writing so much. She told me that she had always wanted to be a writer. She said she had an "active" imagination. I took that as a warning. It has been noted (Durgin, JPPS, XVV, 7) that delusional patients reveal their self-awareness by leading with some mention of their "active" imaginations.

It took several sessions for her to trust me enough to confide in me. After swearing me to secrecy, she described her ongoing affair with a junior faculty member.

This so-called "lover" was someone I knew, though I decided not to mention this fact to her and risk shattering what trust we had established. I know there are disagreements within the therapeutic community about the level of honesty we owe our patients, but I believe that it's an individual call, a decision to be made for every patient.

I arranged a meeting with my colleague and broached the subject as delicately as I could. I wanted to be sure. Readers are directed to my paper ("Belief and Consequence: What

Have We Gained and Lost if Freud Believed Dora?") for a discussion of the metrics of judging the truthfulness versus the fantasies of our patients.

It was a challenge to interview my colleague without violating professional confidentiality. The faculty member denied his involvement, and everything I've learned in my work convinced me that he was telling the truth.

The fantasy of a love affair when there is no love affair is a familiar story.

But this was the point at which Miss L's story took a less familiar turn.

After her delusion evolved to the point at which the professor had (or so she imagined) broken off relations and started an affair with her best friend and classmate—yet another delusion—my patient began to experience bizarre ideations.

She insisted that her dog, her beloved beagle, was not her dog. She claimed that someone had stolen her pet and substituted another beagle who looked just like it. But it wasn't her dog. No amount of persuasion could convince her otherwise.

During several sessions, I tried a version of conditioning—a Hail Mary attempt, I should say. Whenever Miss L began to talk about her stolen pet, I would turn my head and look out the window and try to project boredom, ennui, and disbelief.

Nothing seemed to work. Nothing seemed to mitigate the gale force of her delusion.

From this point on I argued that her family should be notified. The patient was still a minor, and we needed their permission to start her on antipsychotic medication, beginning with the lowest dosage and titrating up as needed.

Do people need to be stopped from hurting themselves? We need to respect their right to self-determination, even when we think we know what would be good for them.

Eventually, she was medicated and obliged to withdraw from college.

The story took yet another turn. She again came to the attention of the school clinicians when she made accusations to the faculty department head, claiming that her dog was being used as an experimental subject in the school's psychology research laboratories. She claimed to have received photographs of her dog in a cage in the lab.

This, too, was a delusion. Admittedly, mice have been used in the past, as subjects, but even that practice had been discontinued along with changing attitudes about humane animal treatment. Certainly dogs had never been used in our research facility. It is widely known that, for genetic and behavioral purposes, beagles make poor experimental subjects.

Even those of us who believe the most unlikely things cannot imagine that anyone would steal a young woman's dog and—for some sinister, improbable, in fact impossible reason—replace it with a look-alike.

The delusion marked the patient's near-total split from reality.

Over time I have lost contact with the subject, but I received a thank-you note from her mother, ten years after our last session. She informed me that her daughter has become a reasonably high-functioning individual.

It's a professional problem, one could say. We doubt the

success of our best efforts. But cases such as Miss L's reassure us
that there is a reason why our intervention is not only helpful
but can actually change lives.

John James Randall
Muller Professor Experimental Psychology
Woodward University

That was where it ended. It seemed impossible that any respectable journal would publish crap like that. Aren't they supposed to check these things? Repeat their results or whatever? Apparently, Dell's cruelty and damage had cured me of my delusions and changed my life for the better. This was the story of my life that would stick, because professors had the power. But it was my life. My life!

There was no one who would listen to me. No way to make my voice heard.

Reading Dell's lying paper had a visual component. Strangely, I didn't picture him or me and what we'd done together.

I saw Professor Muller's puppeteer hands, pulling marionette strings in the background.

Every word of Professor Randall's paper was a lie. Though like all really good, convincing lies, it had an element of truth. Our affair had not been a delusion. It wasn't a dog, but there was a pet involved. Pyewacket! And, yes, I had evidence that my cat had been used in a laboratory experiment. Unless the laboratory scene had been staged and photographed just to torment me. But why?

Was I just a research subject for Professor Randall's paper? If so, he'd reached questionable results. I read his paper until I could read it without bursting into tears. Until it was just another bogus story that another bogus scientist had invented.

I was glad that Holly had accused and exposed him as the predator he was. I wanted to see our former teacher's life ruined the way he'd ruined mine.

I was happy she had written it. Even if she hadn't told the true story, or the whole story. Even if she'd left out the part about her own involvement.

About what they had done to me.

One of the longer articles about Professor Randall's dismissal cited this paper in the journal, which the writer criticized as a text-book case of not believing the woman.

Chapter Twenty-Two

AFTER I got home from the gala dinner, buzzed from the high of poisoning the Woman of the Year, there was no one I wanted to see more than Catzilla.

I opened a bottle of cold white wine. I threw away the cork. I sat in my comfortable chair. I drank one glass, then the next.

Then the next.

My cat jumped up into my lap. I told him about the evening.

I know that talking about my cats has stunted my dating life, but I like describing the sweetness of coming home to Catzilla. It shows me at my best.

No one had wanted him at the shelter. Even as a kitten, there was something a little too tough-guy about him. He already seemed a little fierce, a little spoiled, a little entitled. A bro. You could tell he was going to be big. A muscle cat. A lot of people don't want that. They want something silkier, or fuzzier, cuter, more domestic.

I'd been to the shelter several times, always coming home

empty-handed. By then I knew what to wait for, what to look for: that moment of eye contact. I'd look at a cat, and a cat would look at me, and I'd know. I'd just know. Some people might not believe this. They think that if you want eye contact, you should get a dog.

But that's what happened with Catzilla. We found each other in that shelter. He looked at me; I looked at him.

Catzilla named himself. He grew into his name. He was huge. He looked feral. Muscular and lean. Except that he was gray, he reminded me of a silhouetted black cat arching its back and baring its teeth in a Halloween decoration.

I have always hated the word *stride*, but the first time I brought him home and set him free, Catzilla *strode* into my house, his back rippling, snapping his broad shoulders as if he owned the apartment. And yet he has always been as sweet-natured as a bunny. I've never had a more loving cat, except for Pyewacket, of course.

Catzilla was always happy to see me, always wise enough to give me the space to decompress, to pour my wine and settle into my armchair.

Only then would he jump up into my lap. His weight and warmth and his regular purring soothed me. Under Catzilla's heft, his steady breathing and quietly thumping heartbeat, I could reconsider what I'd done to Holly and decide if I was sorry.

I checked myself for guilt, regret, self-recrimination—nothing. Zip. I'd done nothing worse than what Holly had done to me. Maybe I'd caused Holly a flash of fear, a thrum of illness, a brief public embarrassment. But that was nothing compared to stealing a person's beloved cat and using him in a science experiment.

Tormenting Pyewacket. Tormenting me.

———

Judging from the awe and reverence with which the gala dinner guests watched the Woman of the Year being wheeled out of the restaurant by the EMT squad, everything I'd done had only made her star shine more brightly.

I didn't care. Catzilla didn't care. He understood. He would have wanted me to do the same thing if anyone treated him the way they had treated Pyewacket.

Not that anyone would.

Catzilla can defend himself.

Cats have a gift, especially rescue cats. They've suffered. If they grow to love you, they want to spare you from suffering.

Not long ago I watched a video clip that went viral. A toddler kept grabbing the railing of the balcony of a high-rise apartment. Maybe the kid was planning to climb the railing and fall over the edge—who knows?—but he couldn't. Because the family cat—a large, elegant Siamese—kept gently pressing his claws into the toddler's hands, so that toddler let go of the railing and lost interest.

Who was filming this? Shouldn't that person have intervened before the cat did? Even so, it was my favorite video. I watched it over and over. It replaced all my favorite videos of kittens playing the piano, snuggling with baby pigs, dancing in the shower.

I knew that Catzilla thought as fast and was as smart as the cat that had saved the kid on the balcony. Every day Catzilla kept me away from the railing.

And, of course, he saved my life.

———

The morning after the gala dinner, I googled Holly Serpenta and clicked on *news*. Nothing—except for the announcement, from a few days back, about the Woman of the Year dinner. Well, sure, you wouldn't expect a celebrity's allergy attack to make the front page—not unless it was Brad or Angelina.

Not unless someone died.

I checked the gossip columns, Instagram, and Facebook. Nothing nothing nothing. Maybe someone paid someone to keep it off Page Six.

I assumed it meant that Holly was fine, that she'd recovered without incident. Perhaps they'd made her stay overnight for observation, but now I imagined her home in her beautiful apartment, FaceTiming with her gorgeous half-Italian grown children. Having learned her lesson (not even suspecting what that lesson was), she was—I imagined—publicly reflecting on how her recent near-death experience had reminded her how precious every minute is.

I wondered if her assistants would be fired. I felt a little guilty about that. But they should have thought harder before signing on to work for Holly Serpenta.

Another couple of days went by, during which I played happily with Catzilla and contemplated (less happily) my future.

I was playing with my cat and his mouse toy—encouraging him to unleash the inner hunter that he was too nice to let me see—when someone knocked on my apartment door.

I looked around. Catzilla had ripped the head off the mouse, and puffs of stuffing were scattered on the floor. Too late to clean up now.

I was surprised that someone had gotten through the front door and up the stairs. Maybe a neighbor had buzzed a stranger in.

"Who is it?"

"NYPD," said a male voice.

I'd seen—and heard—this scene play out so many times on

TV that it took a few extra seconds for me to process the fact that it was actually happening. Now. To me.

I flipped the little lever over the peephole. Two men stood outside, their faces distorted by the fish-eye lens. One was white, the other Black.

They looked like TV detectives. But you can never be sure. I'd heard about home invasions committed by criminals impersonating police.

"Can I ask you to show me your badges? Please?" I liked how competent, in control—how sane—I sounded. Though that extra *please* had been a little whiny.

Two shiny badges and IDs appeared just far enough from the peephole so I could see them. They'd done this before. They knew just where and how to hold their IDs.

I unbolted the door and let them in.

Catzilla came trotting over, curious about the first visitor we'd had in a very long time. He more or less blocked the door, defending me, so the detectives had to squeeze past him, never taking their eyes off him, as they entered the apartment. Did I imagine the white detective had his hand on his gun? I saw both of them—trained to see details—take in the headless mouse and the puffs of stuffing.

"Quite a cat you've got there," the white detective said.

"Thank you," I said.

Were they waiting for me to say that Catzilla was harmless? Well, he *was* harmless—but there was no need for them to know that.

Anyway, all I knew was that my cat was harmless to me. I liked them thinking that I was the kind of woman who had a tough male cat.

An attack cat that sprang on command.

I bent down and Catzilla jumped into my arms. I held him close. I would hold him as long as this visit lasted. He would let himself be held. He was company, comfort. Protection. I needed him as a buffer. Body armor.

"I'm Detective Reardon," said the cop from central casting, the white one with the broad, round Irish face, the sharp blue eyes semi-twinkling beneath his high forehead and graying buzz cut.

"And this is Detective Pearson." The Black cop looked even more like a cop on TV, only more handsome. Under normal circumstances, his good looks might have made me self-conscious. Nothing about this was normal.

"Can I help you?" I managed to say.

They looked past me down the corridor.

"Come in. Come into the living room. Have a seat."

Catzilla had shredded the legs of the sofa and the cushions on one of the chairs. If they saw, they didn't care. Probably they'd seen dead people half-eaten by cats.

"May I ask what this is about?"

"We're following up on some leads . . . talking to everyone who attended the Woman of the Year Gala dinner on the eighth. The credit card listings show that you purchased a ticket for a . . ." He checked his notes. "Miranda DeWitt. A friend?"

Well, that was a problem right there. If I told them that there was no Miranda DeWitt, that I *was* Miranda DeWitt, it might have seemed . . . suspicious. But if I sent them looking for Miranda De-Witt, sooner or later they'd find out she didn't exist. A woman by that name had gone to college with me and Holly and died on the slopes of Davos.

I'd take a chance on there being more than one Miranda De-

Witt, and now there was another one: me. "I bought the ticket for my friend Miranda. As a cheer-up present. She's going through a nasty divorce. But she was out of the country that night. At the last minute she decided to leave for Paris. So I figured I'd use the ticket myself. As long as I had it, why not go? Does that make sense?"

"Right," said Detective Reardon uncertainly.

They weren't interested in my story. Shouldn't they have paid attention? Everyone who owns a TV knows that a detective perks right up when he hears about anyone doing anything under an assumed name.

But not this time. Not these guys.

Why was I worried? Why would they suspect me of anything? Just because I attended a party under a fake name. Just because I poisoned the guest of honor? Had someone figured that out?

Everything depended on not sounding anxious as I asked, "Did something happen at the dinner?"

Detective Pearson said, "Not at the dinner. After."

"How long after?"

"There has been a fatality." Detective Reardon sounded hollow, like a bad recording of himself, with interference and an echo.

"That's terrible," I said.

Did Holly not recover? Did the EpiPen not work? Did she go into shock again and . . . was I guilty of murder?

I hadn't meant to kill her.

I didn't want her to die.

Who would believe me? And why was I assuming that something had happened to Holly? There were hundreds of rich and famous people at that dinner. Anyone might have had a misadventure.

A fatality.

"I don't mean to pry—I know it's none of my business—but . . . can you say what happened, or who it happened to . . . ?" I didn't expect an answer. "I know that homicide squads often withhold details that would only be known to the killer. I watch a lot of TV."

I tried to smile. The cops didn't even try.

"Holly Serpenta," said Detective Pearson.

Didn't they hear my heart hammering my rib cage?

"I heard she fell ill at the dinner but . . ."

"She's dead," said Detective Reardon. Why did I think he was enjoying this? Waiting for my reaction.

"Oh my God . . . my God." I was allowed to be upset. *Supposed* to be upset. The Woman of the Year was dead. We'd just come together to honor her.

"I knew she had an allergy attack or something. I mean, that's what everyone was saying. We all saw the EMT squad arrive, and everyone was talking about what happened as they wheeled her out. Was it that? Did her condition worsen or . . . ?"

"She's dead," repeated Detective Reardon. Not challengingly, not monitoring my reaction. Just stating a fact.

"That's terrible." I hid my face in Catzilla's fur. I didn't want them to see my expression. Sadness, surely. But guilt? Personal terror?

I had been playing a prank. A nasty joke, but still. Now I was a murderer. I'd ruined my life—for what? I hadn't meant to kill her. But who would believe that now?

"*Was* it that allergy thing? Was it fatal?"

"What?"

"A fatal allergic reaction?"

The detectives looked at each other. They shook their heads.

"She was strangled," they said. In unison. "Murdered."

Maybe they weren't speaking in unison. Maybe just one of them said it, and I heard an echo inside my head.

"Where?" I said. "Where did she die?

"In her apartment. We think it was someone she knew. Any information you could provide—anything you saw or heard that evening—would be helpful."

I acted as if I was already under suspicion, even under arrest. I talked too fast, too much. I rambled. I had seen at the dinner what everyone else saw at the dinner. The women she had saved. Her beautiful speech. I cried. I went over and introduced myself. We took a picture together, but it didn't show up on my phone. I wasn't good with the camera.

I asked if they had any suspects, but before they could answer, I rattled on about what a tragedy this was. Holly was such a hero, a model for us all, how amazed I'd been at that dinner to hear the range of her accomplishments, only some of which I'd known about.

Detective Reardon yawned.

If the cops were so bored by me, why were they even here?

"Did you personally know Miss Serpenta?"

Did I *personally know*? At another time, I would have told them what *redundant* meant.

"We went to college together, but we'd fallen out of touch. But I've continued to admire her. She is one of my heroes." That was the second time I'd said *hero*. Wasn't that a tip-off? TV villains often repeated themselves. "*Was* one of my heroes. Oh dear God!"

"Right," said Detective Pearson. They exchanged let's-get-out-of-here looks and stood up. I still had Catzilla in one arm, and with the other I hung on to the chair arms and hoisted myself up, like an old person. Maybe that's how I looked to them. A cat lady with her fat tabby didn't fit the profile of the person they suspected of killing Holly.

The killer was probably a man. I sensed that forensics had decided. That explained the cops' lack of interest in me.

Only then did I feel free to wonder who did it. Dell Randall flashed through my mind. He had good reason to hate her. She had gotten him fired from a job he loved. She ended his career. And he'd never been all that stable. What kind of person gaslights someone, kidnaps her cat, substituting a similar cat? What kind of person makes her think that her real cat was being used in lab experiments, then writes a paper in which everything that happened to this person is rearranged and distorted and lied about and described as her disturbed fantasy?

They said they thought it was someone Holly knew. Holly certainly knew Dell. Maybe Dell wasn't just secretive and destructive. Maybe he was diabolical. Maybe his serial abuse had graduated into murder.

It took a moment for me to remember that Dell was dead.

Dell was dead.

He'd fallen off the edge of a mountain.

Or so people said.

Lots of people who were supposedly dead turned out to be alive. You knew that if you watched as much TV as I did.

Holly had hundreds, maybe thousands, of people in her life. Powerful, passionate people who hated her and held her responsible for something that had gone wrong in their lives. The sex trafficker whose captives she'd freed, the abused wife's husband. The drug dealer who went out of business when his neighborhood was cleaned up, thanks to Holly. Why was I supposing that it was someone from her past? Why? Because *I* was from her past. Because our connection—our lack of connection—was all in the past.

All you needed was one crazy, violent person. One resentment. One serious grudge.

Someone had wanted to kill her—and done it.

Poor Holly!

How many times do I have to say that I didn't want her dead?

Detective Reardon gave me his card, which intensified the weird sensation of watching my life on TV.

I thanked him, and they left.

I locked the door behind them. I typed his number into my phone and put it on speed dial, just in case. Then I took Catzilla to the bedroom and lay down on the bed and curled myself around him and got as small as I could.

I cried. I cried for Holly. For how innocent we were, how young we were, for all the time that had passed. I cried for the time we were friends. I cried because, in my secret heart, I had always imagined the scene in which Holly and I became friends again, when everything would be explained and forgiven, and go back to the way it used to be.

Chapter Twenty-Three

I EXPECTED THE detectives to return with more questions. I waited for them, counting the minutes, the hours, the days.

I have never felt so guilty. I had never done anything to feel so guilty about.

Obviously, I didn't strangle Holly. But I had gone to her gala dinner under an assumed name. What if the cops decided that I was harboring an old grudge? Which I had been. I still was.

I'd poisoned her. What are the chances of someone being poisoned and later strangled by someone with no connection to the poisoner?

Or *was* there a connection? The detectives would want to find out.

Holly's murder headlined the evening news. All you could see was crime scene tape, her doorman, a handsome young man emerging from her building, maybe one of her grown children.

Police were talking to "a person of interest"—not me, obviously. The detectives hadn't shown much "interest" in me.

———

When violence happens to someone you know, even someone you haven't seen for a while, even someone you hate—well, let's say, dislike—you feel uneasy. It's as if a vulture has brushed too close to you, and you can still feel the scrape of its wing. Violence creates an atmospheric disturbance. It churns up its own weather.

At moments I was afraid that whoever had come for Holly might be coming for me.

That was not going to happen! Holly's enemies were out of my league. I was flattering myself to think that they knew I existed. I hadn't seen her in twenty years. We moved in different worlds.

But I was the only one who knew that two attempts had been made on her life within a few days, and one try had been successful. I felt a connection with Holly's killer. Even though, as I keep saying, I hadn't wanted her dead.

———

According to the evening news, the police were closemouthed about the case. To the TV detective procedural fan like myself, this was routine. I googled Holly every few days, trying not to check every few minutes, because I believed that our internet activity was randomly monitored. I didn't want to arouse suspicion.

I felt a whole new kind of guilt. I was deeply sorry that I'd ruined Holly's last hours on earth. I hadn't known they'd be her last. I was sorry that she was dead.

———

The next few weeks were pure paranoia. I was looking over my shoulder so constantly that I kept tripping over the same crack in the sidewalk outside my apartment. Once I fell and bruised my forehead, not a good look. I expected Holly's killer to leap out of every doorway, to appear around the corner of the detergent aisle. But why would her killer want to murder *me*? It was vanity, on my part, to think that anyone cared—that anyone knew who I was.

One afternoon I went downstairs to get the mail. Not that I ever got mail except bills and breakup letters from New York State unemployment.

I looked down and found it, laid diagonally across my doorstep:

A single vampire tulip.

That got my attention.

The deep-red petals, the black streak, the fringe. There was nothing else it could be, though I turned it around and around, as if I were hoping it would turn into a rose or a daffodil.

Anything but what it was.

I stumbled back into my apartment, shut and locked the door, and sat on the couch, trembling, until I could collect my thoughts.

I wanted to throw it away. But I put it in a vase and stared at it, as if I could force it to tell me who'd left it at my door.

My first thought was Dell.

I knew it.

Dell wasn't dead.

My fantasies fed on themselves until it began to seem more likely that Dell was alive and that he'd killed Holly.

He was the link. They were the ones who knew about the vampire tulip. She'd left that detail out of her #MeToo story.

His motive for killing Holly was obvious. She'd ruined his career, forced him out of a job he loved, stopped him from doing his bogus research and playing mind games on female students. After the scandal broke, his beloved monster-mentor Professor Muller died. Maybe Dell blamed Holly for Muller's death. Maybe he blamed me. Maybe I wanted to believe that any of this was true. That he remembered me, at all. That he was still alive somewhere, thinking about me.

None of it made sense. But it wasn't impossible. Falling off a cliff in Mexico minimizes the chances of anyone seeing you vanish, of finding your body. Faking his own death would have been easy for a smart guy like Dell.

I imagined the scenario: Dell assumes a new identity, hangs out in Mexico for a while, arranges for a fake passport, new papers, sneaks back into the United States, and murders the woman who ruined his life.

And then he comes after me. I would be harder to find. But thanks to the internet, there are no more secrets. Someone always knows where you are. Why would Dell want to hurt me? Because I might figure out that he'd killed Holly. Because I might tell someone.

My first phone call should have been to the police. I should have told them everything.

But there were things I didn't want them to know, like a syringe full of walnut oil.

I should have told the detectives. Instead I told Catzilla. At night I drank whiskey and then wine, and told my cat the whole story. I always ended with two lines:

I didn't mean to kill her.

Dell is still alive.

The first sentence was true. I almost convinced myself that the second sentence was true, after I'd said it enough.

Now the faceless stalker waiting for me in every dark corner and around every aisle in the supermarket had a face.

Dell's face.

I wondered if I would recognize him. He would have grown older. Was he still handsome? What would I say? It seemed important to separate fact from fantasy—*my* fantasy, to be specific.

Watching those detective shows hadn't been wasted time. I knew how to proceed. That's why they call them procedurals.

I imagined that I was the rookie cop who gets the long list of telephone numbers to call.

But who do you call to find out if someone is really dead? Or just *supposed* to be dead.

And if that person isn't dead—where is he? Do the dead leave forwarding addresses?

I called the psych department secretary at Woodward. The moment I mentioned Dell's name, her tone changed from pleasant to . . . wary. Frightened, even. Why did I want this information? She knew—and I knew—that Dell's dismissal had posed a public relations problem for the department and probably for the whole school.

Was I a pushy reporter writing a #MeToo update? "Infamous Academic Abusers—Where Are They Now?"

She said, "I'm afraid we have no information on that," and hung up. She wouldn't even say his name.

Where was Dell last seen? In Oaxaca. Where he was supposed

to have died. Maybe he'd lived around there and been hiking near his home when he "disappeared."

Finding out about him in Oaxaca, from this distance, was a needle-in-a-haystack situation. But I remember hearing a TV detective say that you could find a needle in a haystack if you examined every stalk of hay. I also remembered something Professor Muller said in class when he was trying to define *serendipity*.

Serendipity, he told us, was like looking for a needle in the haystack and finding the farmer's daughter.

———

I decided to start with the expat community in Oaxaca. Someone would know where he was.

Something else I'd learned from *House Hunters International* on TV. The expat real estate agent knows everyone in town. Not only does the agent help the house-hunting TV couple find the perfect (well, the best possible) apartment, but (if we believe the program) they introduce them to a crowd of instant best friends.

Google listed three real estate agents in Oaxaca. I decided that I'd call all three. I'd say I was a former student of Professor Randall's, who'd just gotten back from years abroad and was shocked by the news of his death. Had they known him? Do they know what happened, exactly?

The first real estate agent had no idea what I was talking about.

The second had moved back to Cleveland.

The third time I got lucky.

Her name was Helen Baylor. She sounded young. Youngish. My age, maybe. Maybe a little younger.

The expat real estate agents on TV often wore kooky accessories, neon-orange spectacles or expensive leather jackets. I pictured Helen in lime-colored eyeglasses and a little black blazer over an embroidered shirt from the *mercado*.

I knew right away from the catch in her voice, the half-beat of hesitation. She'd known Dell.

Helen said, "It was very sad." And only then: "So you are . . . ?"

"Miranda DeWitt," I said. "I was his student. I just got back from Zurich, where I believe he lived and taught before I was there. I was shocked to hear about his death. A classmate gave me your number."

"Gee," said Helen. "I don't remember giving Dell's number to a former student. But that was a stressful time. People were calling. Even reporters. You're not a reporter, are you?"

"No," I said. "I told you. I was his student. He had a great influence on my life. A positive one, I should say."

Helen gave a bitter little laugh. I guessed she knew about Dell's #MeToo problems.

I heard something in the silence, over the surprisingly good connection: Helen had been in love with him. Or at least she'd had a crush on him. Or something. There was something there.

Why was I surprised? Women were drawn to Dell. I certainly had been.

Dell really was a monster. He'd seduced or charmed this real estate agent, who still mourned him. Did I think I was better than Helen? After everything, despite everything, some part of me hoped that Dell was alive.

"Our community felt the loss. Professor Randall was a great addition. He knew so much about . . . people. For a man with his accomplishments, he wasn't stuffy at all. Everybody liked him.

"He was taking a picture. He slipped. Fortunately, he was

with a group. Unfortunately, he was long dead by the time they got help. Before they found someone who could rappel down the mountain and reach him. I mean . . . reach his physical body."

Physical body. Dell's last conquest, or one of them, was a woman who said *physical body*.

"I am so sorry" was all I could say, and then our conversation took another turn. I don't know how it happened, but in the silence I could hear Helen figuring things out. She knew I wasn't Dell's former student returned from abroad. She knew that I'd had feelings for him, just as she had. I'd been in love with that stupid bastard preying on stupider women.

Let's just say it was a heavy moment between me and the real estate agent in Oaxaca.

Another silence fell. Helen wasn't about to break it.

After that she wasn't giving anything away. She was no longer eager to talk about Dell. If I wanted more from her, it would have to be business.

I said, "You know . . . this may not be the perfect time to talk about it, but . . . some friends and I are thinking of buying . . . of going in . . . on a house in Oaxaca. We've been hearing a lot about what a magical place it is."

I invented a group of friends. I pictured friend-groups I'd seen on TV, neighborhood gentrifiers, supermodels, trust fund babies on dream vacations, though those dream situations often ended with a murder. I thought of that Japanese TV show. *Terrace House*.

Business. This was business. Helen's voice lost its mournful edge and got warmer and more engaged.

We promised to talk again soon. She would pull together some listings. By the way, she was pretty sure she had photos of Professor Randall's funeral on her phone that she would be glad to share.

"He's buried in Oaxaca?"

"Yes, I was there. When they laid him away."

I hated her possessive smugness. Like she was the closest, the one who beat out the rest of us, the winner of the contest. She was there when they buried him.

It almost made me glad that Dell was dead.

If he was dead.

I gave Helen my email: Catzilla@gmail.com. I said I would like to see the photos of Dell's funeral. I'd like it very much.

The pictures that arrived showed a wooden coffin heaped with red and orange flowers. It could have been anyone in that box. Dozens of beautiful women, Mexicans and foreigners, were among the mourners.

For just a moment I wondered if Dell and Helen were in this together. Maybe Dell had involved his lovesick expat real estate agent in his mad plot to take revenge on Holly.

Dell had to be alive. Who else could it be? Who else knew about the vampire tulip—and who else had reason to show up on my doorstep?

———

The next couple of days weren't fun. I was extremely nervous. I went outside only when I had to: to empty Catzilla's box, get food, come back. There was no one I could ask for help, no one to tell this story to or explain why I felt that I was in danger.

Again I should have called the detectives with my new suspicions. But again I had my reasons for avoiding police attention.

Chapter Twenty-Four

ONE AFTERNOON, someone knocked on my door. I peered through the peephole.

I saw a hand. A man's hand. Holding a vampire tulip.

The man had positioned the blood-colored flower so perfectly that all I could see was the hand, the flower—and not the face it hid.

It was creepy, seeing a flower and not a person.

As if the flower had knocked on my door. As if the flower had come to see me.

I was sure it was Dell. I was more certain than ever. My heart raced, and my chest felt tight.

If there's one thing that life is generous with, it's occasions for embarrassment, moments so skin-crawlingly awful that just the memory sends you straight to the mirror to check out your own shocked and stupid face.

This is the most embarrassing part of my entire story.

After twenty years, after Dell destroyed me so totally that I had to leave college and abandon my dream career, after he kidnapped my cat and played with my sanity and sadistically sent me photos of my kitty in an animal research lab, after everything that happened since, how *embarrassing* that I was praying that Dell was at my door.

My vision blurred from the strain of trying to peer through the peephole. I blinked.

The flower was gone, and now there was a face. A man's face.

The face floated in and out of focus. A white guy, early thirties. Clean-cut, wearing glasses.

Not Dell.

I wanted to howl with disappointment, but I didn't want to seem weird. Or rude. God, no! A stranger shows up with a rare flower I used to get from my maybe-dead lover of twenty years ago, and I don't want to act surprised.

A long pale face.

I'd never seen him before.

———

The next part is the part I can't explain, though I have been asked by detectives, colleagues, fans, and haters alike.

After the video went viral, people often asked me: Why did I invite the stranger *into my apartment*? How could I do that to my cat? To myself? How could I put us in danger?

Go ahead and judge me, those of you who have never done anything that made absolutely no sense.

To understand, really understand, I would have to be the trained psychologist that I never became. Why did I do something so reckless? Someone had just murdered a woman who, like me, knew about vampire tulips. And I was welcoming a stranger who happened to be holding that particular flower, out of all the flowers on the planet.

Was it my secret death wish? Guilt? What was I guilty about? Holly's death was a tragedy. But my little stunt with the walnut oil wasn't what had killed her.

I have always blamed myself for Pyewacket's disappearance. But how could I have predicted what Dell and Holly would do? I should never have let them into my life. I should have chosen my cat above them. I should have put Pyewacket first.

"Wait one second," I said through the door.

I went and got my phone and slipped it into my pocket. For company. For protection.

I picked up Catzilla. He pressed himself against me. Catzilla wasn't leaving me. My cat would keep me safe.

I opened the door with my other hand.

"Come in," I said. "Come in."

————

My visitor was tall and thin. He wore a dark suit, a white shirt, and a tie. John Lennon glasses, overbright blue eyes. Wound tight. A fanatic's face. A gawky teenage boy lived inside the skinny young man. His pants stopped at his ankles; his neck stuck out of his collar. He looked like he was wearing the clothes of a much older person. Maybe a dead person's clothes.

He looked more like a Wall Street type than a serial killer. Or like a Wall Street–type serial killer. His piercing gaze made me think of a God-haunted country preacher, not that I'd ever met one.

There was an awkward stall in the doorway. Neither of us moved. He pressed his back around the doorjamb and slipped past me with a funny crablike movement so that now I was following him into my own apartment. That was disconcerting. We were long past the moment when I could have slammed the door in his face and locked it.

It was oddly comforting that he hadn't wanted to touch me.

Even so, he was scary. I can say that now. At the time I couldn't admit it. I wanted to find out about the tulip. I wanted to know what he knew about Holly and Dell. Looking back, it seems crazy that I cared about that more than my life. That my curiosity about the past was stronger than my survival instinct.

"Let's sit down in the living room," I said, struggling to maintain some hostess-like control, though by now he was walking ahead of me, which was threatening in itself. It reminded me of the first time Catzilla came home from the shelter, how he strode through the apartment like he owned it. He'd gone straight for the refrigerator and waited till I poured him a bowl of milk. It was as if he'd lived here in a previous life. It crossed my mind, only now, that Catzilla might be a steroidal reincarnation of Pyewacket.

I thought of the Highsmith story about the man and the cat trying to kill each other. If my visitor was dangerous . . . I squeezed Catzilla against me. He shifted his weight to make himself easier to hold.

The stranger left a faint smell of mothballs in his wake. It was like being home-invaded by someone who'd been in storage. He was a head taller than me, bigger and younger and stronger.

I should never have let him in.

I felt for the phone in my pocket. Could I dial 911 without looking? I had Detective Reardon on speed dial.

I told myself I was overreacting. I had no idea who he was or why he was here. He might not be dangerous. There was no need to panic.

I'd let him in because of the tulip and its connection to Holly and Dell. I wanted to know what it meant. That was why I was scared, why I *should* have been scared. Holly was dead. She'd been murdered.

Maybe I *had* seen him before. Maybe I'd seen a photo of him. Maybe he was the unhinged ex-con played by Robert Mitchum in *Night of the Hunter*.

Catzilla didn't like him. I could tell. My cat wouldn't leave my arms, not that I wanted him to. He hissed softly. I said, "Shh." I hoped the stranger didn't hear.

You'd think that my cat would have been interested in a new person. In anyone. But I felt him grow tense and wary. He shifted in my arms, shifted again. He couldn't get comfortable. He didn't want to.

The young man still hadn't introduced himself or explained why he was there. My anxiety bubbled up from under that murky silence. He navigated down the little hall into the living room.

He was edging toward the couch, but the tulip was a problem. He didn't want to put it on the sofa. He wanted to give it to me.

That was what he had come for.

I hoped.

I still had Catzilla in the crook of my elbow when I took the tulip.

Lowering my elbow, I felt for my phone in my pocket.

Was he on drugs? He wouldn't look at me. There was something old-fashioned about him, smudged, like a faded family snapshot.

He perched on the edge of the couch. His legs were jittering, his shiny black shoes drumming the carpet. That didn't seem like a good sign. I thought of a frog in biology lab, hit by an electrode.

That's how he seemed: electric. A regular human third rail. I decided not to alarm him more. *Oh, why had I let him in?*

Decades of being sensible undone in one stupid move.

I went into the kitchen.

I put Catzilla down on the kitchen counter, the only place that he wasn't allowed to be. That was my signal to him that something was unusual. Dangerous. But I don't think he needed the warning. I think he already knew.

I put the tulip in a vase, just as I used to do with Dell. As I'd been conditioned to do. That had been a sexual thing, which was the last thing I wanted this to be.

I still had the same crystal vase. I'd brought it from my college apartment to my parents' house and now here. Was it good or bad luck? It was the only vase I had.

I should have found a way to hide a kitchen knife and take it with me back to the living room. But I was wearing jeans and a shirt, I had nowhere to hide it. And I couldn't imagine a knife fight I could win.

I looked at the tulip and thought of Dell, and I began to cry. Catzilla watched me cry, watched me wash my face and dry my eyes.

I picked Catzilla up with one arm, grabbed the vase with the other hand, and went back into the living room. The stranger was still sitting on the edge of the couch.

Catzilla and I sat down across the narrow room. It was the farthest away from him that I could get—but still uncomfortably close.

"You don't remember me, do you?" he said.

Was it someone I'd fired at Cobrox? I recalled so little of what had happened in that office. So many features merged into one unhappy face.

How ironic, to spend twenty years protecting the company from murderous former employees, and now that I'd left the job, my very own disgruntled former employee had come to find me.

This wasn't about my job. The tulip was about Dell.

And Holly.

"I'm Otto," he said, and stood up and crossed the room and bent over to shake my hand. He moved in a strange way, scurrying, but slightly creaky, like a cross between a chipmunk and a large water bird. "Otto Muller."

That had been my evil professor's name. Professor Muller was dead.

He backed up and sat down again.

"That's the name on my birth certificate. My parents told me they changed it to Paul. But it was always Otto. After they died, I reclaimed my name. I didn't have to do much. They never actually changed it. They just told me they did. It was always there. On the books. Waiting for me. Otto waiting for Otto. I like it that my names spells the same frontwards and backwards, don't you? My sister's name was Anna, also fully reversible."

"Otto," I said. Of course. Professor Muller's son, grown now. The little boy who'd fainted. The failed eugenics experiment.

"Thanksgiving," I said.

"Bingo," he said.

"I'm Lorelei." He knew that.

A line from the Beatles chimed stupidly in my mind. All you have to do is act naturally.

The couch was between me and the door. I wondered how I could get past him.

He jackknifed forward. I smelled mint on his breath. Then he sank back against the pillows.

"You know," he said, "it's always strange when the children know more than the grown-ups. Even my sister and I, who were raised to know more than most grown-ups, a lot more. Okay. Where do I begin? When you walked into our dining room that Thanksgiving, you thought we were the Addams family, right?"

That was *exactly* what I'd thought.

"The Addams family. Only not funny. Not funny at all. You thought my sister and I were too terrified or beaten down to do anything but mumble hello. You couldn't have known that we were trying not to giggle."

"At what?"

"At the fact that we knew you, and you didn't know us. You thought you were seeing one thing, but you we were seeing another. We had an edge on you. You were meeting us for the first time, but we knew all about you.

"Father used to take my sister and me to sit behind the one-way glass and watch you in class. Those were our field trips with Father. It was boring, but we enjoyed the attention—some real, some fake—we got from Father's faculty and staff."

"*You* were there?" I said. "Behind the glass?"

His face set. "Afterward, we discussed you with Father."

It shocked me that there were kids behind the glass. They didn't belong there! Had we known, we might have felt less free to talk about sex and love, our dreams, heartbreak, and ambitions—in front of children.

Maybe Otto was making it up. Maybe he knew something about that classroom and knew that I'd been a student. His father had been all-powerful. Even so, it seemed unlikely that the faculty and the school would allow children in that room. I remembered looking at the one-way glass and wanting to see through it. To see

if anyone suspected my relationship with our teacher. It never occurred to me that the eyes belonged to a boy and his sister.

"The spying part was fun at first," Otto said. "Until it wasn't. You
know, there was this Japanese TV show, *Terrace House*, where they
put a bunch of twentysomething men and women in a house to
gossip and flirt and torture one another. Then older semi-celebrities
analyze the goings-on and laugh at the kids in the house."

"I've watched that show!" Weirdly, this reassured me. We were
having a normal conversation about TV!

He laughed, harder and longer than he should have, when he
realized that I wasn't laughing.

"All of you spoiled college students bitching about this and
that. Why would a child care? My sister and I played little games
trying to cut the boredom. Who is your favorite student? Which
one do you like or hate? I liked you the best."

I didn't know how to respond. It felt wrong to say thank you.

"I always chose you because you were the prettiest. And because you were fucking the professor, who worshipped Father. We
talked about it with Father. You didn't talk as much as the boys,
but what you did say seemed . . . brave. We knew a few things
about you before that Thanksgiving. A few big things. Though
maybe they seem smaller now."

"They never seem small," I said.

"I thought not." Otto clasped his arms above his head and
stretched as if he were trying to work out a knot in his back. I
could feel Catzilla tense.

"The strange thing was that as my sister and I got older, you
students stayed the same age. We'd hear the same stories from kids
who thought they were the first ones ever. But every so often we'd
hear something that made us stop and pay attention.

"Like when you told the class that someone stole your cat and replaced it with a cat that looked just like it. That made a big impression."

"It happened," I said.

"Oh, I'm sure. I believed you. I'd overheard your professor friend telling Father about your pathological attachment to your cat. Father said that humans had been conditioned to love animals, but it was a fragile bond. His theory was that humans could hardly tell one animal from another. We, of course, had no pets. We weren't allowed to. Not even a turtle.

"Your teacher said that people love their pets.

"Father said, 'Perhaps we can design an experiment that would push this question further. Do you really think that your friend would be able to tell her cat from a cat that looked just like it?'

"When you told the class that someone stole your cat and replaced it with a look-alike, I thought back to Father's conversation with your lover. Former lover by then. At the time, my sister said, 'The teacher dumped the blond one and now he's fucking her friend with the freckles.'

"Holly," I said.

"The future Holly Serpenta," said Otto.

When he said her name, I knew.

When he said her name, I knew he had killed her. I heard an off note, a tremor, an undertone in his voice. I knew, and I didn't want to know. I told myself I was wrong. How could you figure out something so serious from a couple of words?

Just then he started rooting around in his jacket pocket.

Why did I wonder if he had a weapon? What had made me think that?

Catzilla wondered too. Every muscle quivered.

I couldn't speak for a while. Then I heard myself say, "Does your sister live . . . nearby?"

"My sister is dead," he said. "A suicide. A disease to which our family seems genetically predisposed."

"I'm sorry," I said.

After that, neither of us said anything for a long time.

"I remember that you fainted," I said, just to end the silence that seemed likely to last forever. I'd said the most awkward possible thing.

"I still don't know how my father did it. Hypnosis, maybe. I was a suggestible child, more so than my sister. Another thing he hated about me. He made us watch a nature film about fainting goats. He taught me how to faint and he taught us to make that snort."

"He bent and shaped us, like bonsai. I am the child raised in the box with levers to pull to get treats. I was the experiment they shouldn't have done on mice. There was no punishment outright, no physical cruelty, but sometimes there was no food and always serious disapproval."

I put my hands over my ears. I didn't want to think that he and I had something in common besides watching the same TV show. We had both been used as lab animals in unethical experiments. And we had conflicted feelings about the mad scientists who experimented on us.

"Are you all right?" he asked. "You look sad. Or something."

"Fine," I lied.

He smiled. His teeth were unnaturally white.

"You mean, 'I am fine.' I'm sure you remember that Father and my weakling, furious bitch mother made us speak in full sentences."

I noticed that he'd used the word *bitch* about two different women. He wanted me to notice. He wanted me not to like it.

Things had taken a turn.

"I'm sure you remember how Father made things hard for Mother, the grotesquely undercooked turkey, the dull carving knife. Turning the ordinary nightmare of the holiday into a really special, really extraordinary nightmare. You do remember, don't you, Lorelei?"

I nodded.

"You thought you knew so much. So very, very much. But you knew nothing, really. You were so infatuated with my father's phony, sycophantic-little-bitch protégé."

It shocked me to hear Dell described like that. But I liked it, in a way. That was what Dell was, what Dell had been. I liked hearing someone say it.

"What's funny?" Otto said.

"Nothing," I said. "Nothing's funny."

"Nothing is. Nothing was. That Thanksgiving, I was fascinated by you. Absolutely transfixed. More than all those times I'd watched you in class."

"With me?" I couldn't help it that a compliment still pleased me a little.

"Not exactly *with* you." He snapped his lips shut like a lizard. "I was obsessed with how you saw *me*. I don't know how to say this, but I felt, it was as if you were . . . as if you knew what I was feeling. You didn't just know it. You felt it. Every time Father spoke, you and I felt the same thing. It was like you and I had achieved some kind of mind meld."

"Mind meld?"

"I used to read a lot of science fiction. I stopped. It seems too real."

Mind meld had an invasive stalker edge. I decided to ignore it.

"Want to know a secret?" he said.

I felt stuffed to the gills with secrets. "Sure."

"I didn't really faint. I faked it. I'd fainted plenty of times before. For real. Father made me faint all the time. He could do it just by looking at me. Everything would go very bright, glittery, and I would get sleepy and very, very . . . heavy. Like I weighed a million pounds. But that time wasn't real. I faked it. I wanted you to know that Father could make me faint. I wanted to know how you felt when you saw it."

"I thought it was real."

"I'd had practice."

"And how did I feel?"

"You? You felt freezing cold."

How did he know? Had he seen me shiver? He'd been on the floor with his eyes closed.

"I'm right," he said. "Aren't I?"

"I guess so," I said.

"We're two of a kind. We are."

"I don't know about that," I said.

"You probably felt sorry for my mother, sawing away at the raw turkey. But she was his willing accomplice. Later she committed suicide, so there is always that. Not the greatest way to apologize to me and my sister for our lab-rat-nightmare childhood. Suicide was a brilliant idea Father got from her. It's like they committed a double suicide that took ten years."

What could I say? I thought about that Thanksgiving. How young and uncertain I'd been. How self-involved. I didn't believe we were two of a kind. A crazy light glinted off his glasses, off his scrubbed-shiny cheeks.

"I assume you heard about Father's death."

"I read something," I said. "In the papers."

"You read bullshit," he said so loud that Catzilla startled and dug his claws into my side. "The official story was heart attack. But that's not what happened.

"After your friend Holly destroyed him and his department and left an indelible stain on his brilliant work, for no good reason except more publicity for herself, he sank into a depression. I don't know where he got the idea of going on a safari. I think he may have met a woman . . . I never knew. Someone told him about it, or someone persuaded him to go on a luxury wildlife tour of Africa. A retirement present to himself."

Otto scooted forward so his knees were closer to mine.

He pulled a large carving knife out of the pocket of his jacket. How did that fit in there? Why didn't it make a hole in his coat?

I'd been right to be afraid. He really was going to kill me. Why would you pull a knife on someone unless you planned to hurt them? Or at least were thinking about it.

Even then I didn't believe that I was about to die. It still felt like a dream of death, from which you wake, only to keep dying.

He went on in the same tone, as if a knife weren't an extra element added to the conversation.

"It was one of those misadventures. Happen every so often. The companies are insured. A mountain gorilla went mad and tore up the camp. Father's tent fell in on him, injuring his arm. The animal was shot."

Otto's voice got louder and higher. "Can you honestly for one minute tell me that there isn't a God? That the law of karma doesn't operate, that Father wasn't being paid back for what he did to those animals in that lab? Was it just a coincidence?"

Spit was flying from Otto's mouth. When he talked about his father, which was *all* he talked about, he swung between hatred and worship.

"No. I wouldn't say that."

"Say what?"

"That it was coincidence."

I thought of Dell playing video games with the monkeys. What if everything that happened since, including my possibly being killed by Professor Muller's son, happened because I just stood there? Because I stood there and watched the caged monkeys doing the tricks they'd learned the hard way? I did nothing. I thought it was cool.

Was that bad enough to die for?

"Father was never the same. Six months after his return he went to his hunting cabin and ate two bottles of pills. It was a week before anyone found him. Any humans, I mean. There were animals involved there, too. Chapter two in the animal kingdom's revenge on Father. A coda, you could say."

I struggled not to imagine animals gnawing on Professor Muller's corpse, which meant I imagined it.

"I'm sorry." I'd lost count of how many times I'd said that.

"I don't think so, "Otto said. "I don't think you are. And why should you be sorry? Should I blame you for not speaking out when a grown man makes his little son faint by looking at him? Like some evil party trick? For not speaking up when a father describes his only son as a failed science experiment? For saying nothing, for doing nothing, for minding your own business, for not wanting to embarrass anyone—"

Otto slid his glasses down his nose and rubbed the bridge of his nose, then pushed them up and winced. "Your famous friend

Holly destroyed him. A harsh, merciless light was shone on his work. On everything he achieved."

The father who made him talk in complete sentences. The father who taught him to faint on command. Sitting there in front of me was a semi-brainwashed human being! After everything his father had done, he still believed he was a genius.

"The only time we were allowed to play video games was when we played with the monkeys. I hated the smell of the animal labs. The smell of their fear and death and—"

"I know," I said. "I was there."

He wasn't having any of it. No fellow feeling between us, no shared common experience of the terrifying lab. "Your friend Holly got the lab shut down."

His voice got dark when he said *your friend Holly*. I wished he'd stop calling her that.

"It wasn't Holly's fault. It would have happened anyway. It's a different time."

Why was I defending the woman I'd tried to poison? Because I didn't want his anger at her spilling over onto me.

"My father was brilliant. You know he consulted for the government. Through several administrations. There was always a place at the president's table for an expert on mind control. He was an intelligence hero. After the war, they spirited him out of Europe because they saw what he could do."

Had Professor Muller really been a Nazi? We'd called him one. We'd thought it was a joke. I needed time to think about this. But this was not the moment.

"Father paid us to play with the monkeys. We were forbidden to play video games any other time. He said he was conditioning us to do what we loved and get paid for it. Like he did."

"Did it work?" I said.

"Not at all. It only works if you know what you love."

Otto pulled back his cuff and lightly pressed the knife blade against his wrist. Looking straight at me, he laughed.

A tremor went through Catzilla, then another. He was on it. His presence made me feel almost safe, but maybe I only say that because I know what happened.

"Your friend started the avalanche that buried my father." Otto kept bringing the subject back to Holly. I needed to distance myself.

"That was years after I saw her."

Not counting the dinner. I wasn't going to mention that.

For a few moments I almost told him. If he was going to kill me, I had nothing to lose. And it might be interesting to see how it felt to say it. Maybe hearing I'd tried to kill Holly would change his mind about me. The enemy of my enemy is my friend.

"Do you know what set me off? Seeing her face on the cover of the alumni magazine that I still get even though everyone in my family is dead and I didn't even go there. It followed me from place to place and in and out of several serious relationships."

Somehow I doubted about the relationships, but so what? At this point it didn't matter what he said about his life.

"I get the alumni magazine too," I said. "I didn't graduate. They're persistent. They track you down. They think we might have money and want to give it to them. Hilarious."

"They helped me track you down. And then I saw on the college website that your friend Holly was being honored as the Woman of the Year. The woman who killed Father and destroyed his legacy. I couldn't stand it anymore. I needed to do something."

That's what had set me off too. Yet another thing not to bring up. Otto was never going to believe that he and I were on the same side.

"I know what you mean," I said.

"I don't think you do. By the way, it was Father's idea to switch out your cat with another cat. The first test of loyalty that my father and your professor made your friend Holly do was to locate the cat that looked like your cat. It must have been a challenge."

I thought of how I'd gone back to school and confronted the professor. I remembered the smug little smile on his face as he took me around the lab. It wasn't just an experiment to him. It was research—and a joke.

———

Twenty years had passed, and never, not once, had anyone believed my story about Pyewacket. Never, not once, had anyone thought I hadn't imagined it. There were so many things I wanted to ask. Did he know what happened to Pyewacket? Had my cat been caged in the lab? Had someone brought him to a shelter or . . . ?

"Shut up," he said, though I hadn't spoken. "You really need to shut up now. I watched you tell the class about what happened. I watched them think you'd gone crazy. I was the only one who knew you were telling the truth. There was nothing I could do. My sister hadn't heard Father suggest that stunt with your cat. So I didn't tell her about it. It would only have made her more unhappy.

"I was trained to remember. We were Father's memory project. You'd think kids would have hated our home life, hated how he treated us, but that would have been like hating oxygen. You know who Father's favorite writer was?"

"No." I expected someone German.

"Borges," Otto said. "All those twists and turns and philosophical mind fuck." He shook his head. Sparkles of light shot off his glasses.

I said, "Your glasses were thicker when you were a child."

"Right. Well, how about that? He had glasses made with the wrong prescription, and he made me wear them when I was bad. Everything got fuzzy. The floor came up to meet me. Nauseating. I used to vomit. That was the kind of punishment. Not physical, but physical. He was always diagnosing me, fine-tuning his diagnosis. He said I was a sociopath."

Okay, then. Otto had said it. A sociopath was sitting in my living room, holding a knife.

"He was wrong," I said. "Wasn't he?" It made no sense, how calm I was. Everything seemed to be happening somewhere to someone else.

"My father was thrilled to identify my sociopathic tendencies, and he set out to see if my condition was *hardwired*—a word I despise—or if it could be changed."

A funny robotic twang had crept into Otto's voice. He sounded like a person who had been grown in a test tube.

"Tendencies?" My voice echoed louder than I would have liked. My visitor had confessed to being a sociopath, and I worried I might be shouting. I wondered how I could get past him if he got up and lunged at me. It was better to keep him talking. I shut my eyes. I needed to keep my thoughts in my head. When I opened my eyes again, he was staring at the tulip.

"The vampire tulip. My God. That was Father, too. Maybe you didn't notice, or maybe he didn't have them that Thanksgiving, but Father always had a vase of them on the sideboard.

"I don't know where he got them. He must have had a supplier. I like to think he spent government mind-control money on exotic flowers. He told the young men who hung around him—there were never any women—that the tulips were a way to make women fall in love with them. By which I assume he meant to make women fuck them. He said the tulips were a visual aphrodisiac, a shortcut around all the tedious things men had to say and pretend in order to get women into bed."

"That's so sexist," I said.

"You think so?" said Otto. "Every time your favorite professor left our house, he'd take one of the tulips. Father would call after him, 'Have fun!' Is there anything more repellent?"

"Your father said all this in front of you?"

"We heard everything. Nothing was kept secret, and everything was kept secret."

Otto got up and swayed a little, then sat down again. I wondered if he might be high, and if that made things better or worse.

After a while he said, "All right, then. Ahem. Has the confessional moment come?"

"I don't know," I said.

"It has. It's the confessional moment. So here it goes. I had to kill your evil friend. I owed it to Father. After she wrote that lying letter, the department fell apart. The lab had been shut down for a while, but Father was stripped of his emeritus title, and two months later he died. Must I refer you to the online discussions of so-called broken heart syndrome?

"I always wanted to know what happened to you. After I killed your friend Holly it became more urgent. If I was going to go to jail, I wanted to see you again. Then I decided I didn't want to go to jail. So now I'm afraid I'm going to have to kill you because I've told you that I killed her."

I was astonished at how calmly I took this bad news.

I said, "When did you change your mind?"

"Just now. Talking to you."

"How did you find me after all this time?"

He laughed. "It took about five minutes to hack into the Woodward alumni directory."

"And why did Holly let you into her apartment?"

"Questions, questions, question. I suppose I'd be asking them too. I showed your friend Holly the tulip. It works every time. Doesn't it? Father was right about that."

I laughed. From embarrassment, maybe.

The tulip had worked its magic on Holly. She hadn't forgotten Dell. That was useful to know, but less important now that she was dead and I might also be dead soon.

He said, "Oh, I almost forgot. I brought something I want you to read."

I felt, through my skin, Catzilla's growl. He growls at cat-food commercials on TV. It's not a friendly hello. It's the sound of a tomcat fighting for the last cat food on the planet.

From the other inside jacket pocket Otto took out a sheaf of papers.

"Read this," he said. "Now."

Catzilla sat in my lap as I read. As I tried to read. At first I couldn't figure it out.

Otto said, "It's a printout from your friend's computer. I figured out her password."

"What was it?" I couldn't help asking.

"Womanoftheyear123! Typical. Bitch! Her assistants must have updated after the dinner was announced."

Another time, I might have laughed. But nothing seems all that funny when someone's holding a knife.

"I searched her files. I found her first draft of that #MeToo story that ruined Father's work. Obviously, someone shortened it before it ran in the paper. I thought you might be interested in what she had to say about you. Her editor made her cut that part. For length. And maybe the lawyers advised it."

On the pages, the letters were still refusing to organize themselves into words.

"I am," I said. "I am interested."

"Then goddamn read it," he said. "It's the same and different from whatever you read."

MY STORY, BY HOLLY SERPENTA
Rough Draft 1

My #MeToo story is so much less horrifying and painful than what so many sisters suffered. I almost hesitate to add it to the gut-wrenching accounts of sexual violence, cruelty, and intimidation.

I know I that my readers, my fans, my friends out there will think that if anyone has moved on past trauma, Holly Serpenta has. But it never goes away. I dream about it. It marked me. My abuser ruined my life. Though in a way, he did me a favor. It took me a while to see that. Women should make our own choices, not because some man tries to destroy us.

So here goes:

I looked up. Otto was watching me read. "I know all this," I said. "Everyone does," said Otto. "Read the goddamn rest."

When I was in college, John James "Dell" Randall, my psychology professor at Woodward University, pressured me into having a sexual affair if I wanted to pass his course and graduate from college. From certain things I'd said in his cultlike group therapy class, he knew that my parents couldn't afford another term. If I didn't graduate that spring, I never would.

Predators go for the wounded.

When I accuse him, I hear two voices. One is my own, and one is the voice of my college best friend, who doesn't wish to come forward, a decision I respect.

Professor Randall was a serial predator. He destroyed her before he destroyed me. Or tried.

I watched helplessly as she fell under his spell. I watched her sanity unravel as he played with her mind.

Otto said, "Did you get to the good part?"

"I guess this is it." When I'd I read the original version in the papers, I was upset because Holly wrote me out of the story. And now I was back in the story again, but it was all a lie.

Anyone who has had a delusional friend or loved one will know how helpless I felt. My best friend became convinced that our professor—first her abuser, then mine—stole her pet cat and replaced it with a cat that looked exactly like it.

I was the first person she told this to. I didn't know what to do. When she repeated her story in class . . . that's when we knew that something was very wrong.

Why would someone replace her cat with a look-alike? Who would go to the trouble?

It was a desperate cry for help.

Our abuser had so damaged my friend that she left college. Her parents came and got her. This intelligent girl spent time in treatment, which succeeded, though relapses have occurred.

Relapses? I should have killed her. Someone else got to it first.

Our college friendship never recovered. At one point she decided that I was involved in the theft of her cat. She accused me of aiding our abuser in subjecting her cat to scientific experiments.

Even in her madness, how could she think I would do that? My friend had gone crazy after being abused by the same man who abused me. She just wasn't as lucky as I was.

I don't know how many other women Professor Randall harmed. But I don't think he stopped with me.

Others in his department knew about the abuse and said nothing.

The rest was pretty much what I had read.

"What do you think?" said Otto.

"It's all lies," I said.

"Not *all* lies. *Some* lies."

"She made it sound ridiculous. The idea of someone stealing a cat and substituting another."

Otto said, "I'm sorry, because you're not as bad as your friend. But I can't have killed her without now killing you. You're both part of my father's story. It's time for that story to end. Think of yourself as the second step in a kind of . . . cleanup operation."

He was talking about my life and death as a cleanup operation.

He stood and came toward me. Holding the knife.

Catzilla jumped out of my arms.

I grabbed my phone from my pocket and started filming.

With more technical know-how than I'd shown in my life, I managed to keep filming while I called the police.

———

Like millions of viewers worldwide, I've watched the clip over and over. Like most of them, probably, I still catch my breath each time Catzilla vaults through the air like a cat shot from a cannon and sinks his fangs and claws in the neck of my attacker. The world steps back with me, a few paces, so I can point the phone at the floor, where now a young man in a dark suit lies curled up, yelling, "Help me somebody help me," while fending off my cat, screaming first from fear and then from pain.

I zoom in on Otto's hand, holding the knife, and stay there until he drops it. I shoot a good ten seconds of the knife flying across the floor and lying where he can't reach it while he's fighting off Catzilla. My phone hand is shaking, but that makes the footage more believable and dramatic. The film gets blurry as I reach down and pick up the knife. I didn't know what I'd do with it, but I liked being the one who had it.

Landscape focus on Otto and the cat. They have reached a standoff. Catzilla has his back up. If Otto moves, Catzilla pounces until Otto goes limp.

My power was at 48 percent, so I turned the phone off and turned it on again when the cops arrived.

By then Otto had crawled into a corner, where he'd stayed, guarded by the cat and me with the knife, though I didn't intend to use it.

Four detectives came this time. Two squad cars twirled their lights, striping my street blue and red. Under different circumstances, I might have thought it looked pretty. Under these, I thought it looked gorgeous.

I watched them take the scene in, or try to: Otto cowering on the floor, Catzilla snarling and hissing. The two I hadn't met pulled their guns but didn't know where to point them. If I hadn't called Detective Reardon, if he hadn't answered, if I hadn't reported that I was being attacked by a man, they might have shot Catzilla. That would have ruined my life again, ruined again by the son of the man who had ruined it the first time. Or maybe the cops would have shot me. I was the one with the knife.

As they watched, I put down the knife and knelt and scooped up Catzilla. The snarling beast turned back into my big darling house cat.

"That's some cat you got there," said Detective Reardon.

They were all looking at Catzilla. I had to redirect them to Otto, who had stayed where he was. I told them Otto was harmless. I begged them to be gentle. Otto didn't resist. I felt sorry for him, but what could I do? He'd told me he'd killed Holly and he was going to kill me.

After the two cops took Otto away, presumably out to the squad car, I showed the film on my phone to the remaining detectives.

Both of them whistled. "Jesus Christ," they kept saying. Detective Pearson told me to be sure and save it as evidence.

"Why would I delete it?" I said. "It's historic."

You'd think I would have been more shaken up. Did that seem suspicious? Many times, on cop shows, trauma victims seem eerily calm.

"You ought to post it on YouTube," I heard Detective Reardon say. Then he said, "I didn't say that. Did anyone hear me say that?"

"Say what?" said Detective Pearson.

I liked these guys, this time around. They respected Catzilla. They admired what he'd done. I hardly minded that their interest in Catzilla's pet trick was already waning.

The reason I didn't care was that I had a little something else to give them that would dramatically change the entire scenario.

I said, "I guess I should have told you sooner. But okay, this is major. While he was here, Otto Muller—the guy on the floor—confessed to the murder of Holly Serpenta."

"Was it credible?" Why was Detective Reardon asking *me*?

"Did you believe him?" asked Detective Pearson.

"I know what credible means," I said. "But yes. Yes, I did. We were all friends from college. That is, Holly and I were friends."

I was trying to remember what I'd told them about Holly the other time they came. I was too jumpy to recall.

The part about Holly hadn't sunk in for them. I knew it would, in a minute.

"Otto was the son of one of our professors. He was just a kid. But he was always around the department. So we knew him. We thought he was weird, one of those weird faculty kids, but kind of cool. He was kind of like a . . . pet. A pet child."

It was thrilling, how easily lying came. It felt like taking off in a balloon. But from now on I would have to be more careful. It's harder to remember what you say when it isn't true.

I said, "He blamed Holly for his father's death. After her #MeToo essay."

Detective Reardon shut his eyes. "The first #MeToo revenge murder. We've been waiting for this shoe to drop."

"I thought we looked into that," said Detective P. "That guy she accused died in Mexico."

That seemed like the final word. Dell was really dead. Actually, I'd known that. I'd just needed to hear a cop say it.

I said, "Not that professor. Another professor. That one's boss. Also named Otto Muller. Senior. This is the son. Holly knew this Otto, from years ago, when he was a kid. That's why she let him into her house."

More lying, but it didn't matter.

Everything had changed.

This was no longer a cat video. Crazy cat lady rescued by her pet.

This was the solution to an unsolved celebrity murder.

"I'm calling forensics," said Detective Reardon.

"For sure," said his partner.

Did I want to go to the hospital? Did I want to come down to the station? Did I want to rest up, and they could come tomorrow and get my statement?

I chose the final option. All Catzilla and I wanted was a little peace and quiet.

It was quite a while before the apartment was peaceful again. Forensics ruined everything and took forever.

I considered phoning the vet to make sure that Catzilla hadn't contracted a disease from biting and scratching Otto. But Catzilla showed me that he was fine. He bounded from table to table, onto the chairs, onto the kitchen counter, where he still wasn't allowed. He smiled when I swatted him away.

I opened a bottle of Burgundy and drank it in half an hour.

————

The video of Catzilla cornering Otto would have had a YouTube life. But the connection to Holly boosted it onto the mainstream news and all over social media.

Holly's death made Catzilla immortal.

Millions of people worldwide watched the clip over and over.

Catzilla and I were famous.

I got used to doing interviews. It seemed important to stay sober. I got stricter about my drinking. It wasn't as hard as I'd heard. That was another way that Catzilla probably saved my life, though I don't like to think about that.

I changed the story a bit. I left out the walnut oil. I warmed up my friendship with Holly and kept it on a low flame throughout the years of our separation. I made it seem as if Otto still thought of us as a team, the way we were in college. In his obsession he'd believed that if he killed one of us, he had to kill the other.

Every so often a hardworking journalist thought to ask me if I had any response to Holly Serpenta's #MeToo statement, and if I'd made any connection between her murder and her statement, even though the killer wasn't the man she'd accused.

I explained that he was the son of the boss of the man she had accused. I said there was way too much violence, especially violence against women.

Sometimes I felt the interviewers were rushing me so they had more airtime for Catzilla's video. Really, I preferred that. I could watch it forever, and I knew that viewers preferred it to a boring talking head me.

It always featured the warning that some viewers might find the images disturbing. Apparently, not everyone found them too disturbing. Not people who worked for large companies, not people who went to meetings in fancy high-rise boardrooms.

Pretty soon my inbox blew up, as the kids say, with inquiries offering me paid product endorsements, mostly for cat food and flea powder and such.

Just as I was deciding on the going price I would ask for me and Catzilla, I got an email and then a follow-up call from the American Feline Protective Society. They asked if I had time to come in and talk to them about forging some sort of association, even about my coming to work for them.

That interview went well. I talked about my cats. I projected the image of the educated, passionate cat lover and not a crazy cat lady. I knew better than to mention Pyewacket having been stolen and replaced with his double. I certainly didn't say anything about my attempt to poison the late, great Holly Serpenta.

Chapter Twenty-Five

THE CATZILLA video changed everything.

My consolation for everything that's been difficult in my life greets me each time I walk into the lobby of the American Feline Protection Society.

On my way to my corner office.

Hello from the receptionists, the secretaries, my colleagues, and hello from my bosses.

Hello, Lorelei! Hello!

Behind the reception desk is a poster of a giant thermometer. The "mercury" rises according to the number of cats that we have saved from cruelty, wrongful imprisonment, and premature death.

I still do the occasional interview, often at the end of newscasts when they show the kind of happy pet adoption or reunion story that makes their audience feel better.

I say that animals are amazing. If I have an extra few seconds, I say that I am grateful to my cat, Catzilla, to the detectives, and to the video technology that has given both Catzilla and me a second life.

I say how grateful I am to be carrying on the kind of rescues performed by my late friend Holly Serpenta, only with cats, not women. Cats need rescue, too.

Tears well up in my eyes when I say that I wish a cat like mine could have been there to save Holly.

———

The trial of Otto Muller for the murder of Holly Serpenta spiked another blast of interest in my Catzilla rescue video.

Because of Otto's attempted attack, the prosecution wanted to call me as a witness. When the defense learned that I had witnessed a traumatic episode from Otto's childhood, they wanted to call me for their side.

In the end, neither side called me as a witness. They had trouble finding a juror who hadn't seen, or heard about, the Catzilla video, and they decided to focus on Otto's fatal interaction with Holly rather than his visit to me.

I didn't attend the trial. I was glad to be spared the ordeal. Even so, I was disappointed to be deprived of the chance to enter my story—the true story, or at least most of it—into the public record.

I would have liked a chance to say that I have forgiven everyone, forgiven everything that happened to me. Granted, it was a bumpy road, but that road led me to finding my true vocation, working in an organized and effective way on behalf of the creatures I love most in the world.

Maybe it seems strange to say, but I feel fortunate, in the way that Holly described in her #MeToo essay. It just took longer for me to find that sense of contentment.

I have made many dear and treasured friends through my job. Sometimes we meet for dinner after work, and every so often we share a pizza and watch an old movie on Sunday afternoons. I have moved so I live closer to the office, and Catzilla and I share a sunny and spacious apartment in downtown Manhattan. Lately I have begun to have lunch with a widowed veterinarian who seems like a truly nice man. He shares my love of cats, four of which he inherited from his late wife.

And here is the best news of all: As a result of my work on behalf of feline protection, I have been named the PETA Woman of the Year. This spring, I will be honored at the organization's annual Gala Dinner in the presence of so many other animal-loving luminaries.

All I had to do was trust my cat to arrange a happy ending for my story.

People say that cats have nine lives. We know that humans have only one.

My secret hope is that Catzilla and I will find a way to split the difference.

Acknowledgments

Emily Bestler and Lara Jones, thank you so much for your skill, your patience, your intelligence!